LIFE
skills

LIFE
skills

Marlis WESSELER

COTEAU BOOKS

All stories © Marlis Wesseler, 1992.

All rights reserved. No part of this book covered by the copyrights hereon may be reproduced or used in any form or by any means—graphic, electronic, or mechanical—without the prior written permission of the publisher. Any request for photocopying, recording, taping, or information storage and retrieval systems of any part of this book shall be directed in writing to CanCopy, 214 King Street West, Suite 312, Toronto, Ontario M5H 3S6.

These stories are works of fiction. Names, characters, places, and incidents either are the product of the author's imagination or are used fictitiously. Any resemblance to actual persons, living or dead, is coincidental.

Some of the stories in this collection have been previously published or broadcast: "The Wall" in Grain, 1987, and in *Out of Place* (Coteau Books 1991); "Whale Watching" on CBC Radio's "Ambience," 1987; "The Gift" in *NeWest Review*, 1988 and in *Sky High* (Coteau Books 1988); "June's Night" in *The Old Dance* (Coteau Books 1986); "Indecent Exposure" workshopped as a prize-winning monologue in Twenty-Fifth Street Theatre's First Annual Short Play Writing Contest, 1988, and in *200% Cracked Wheat* (Coteau Books 1992); and "Life Skills" on CBC Radio's "Ambience," 1990 (in a play version).

Edited by Edna Alford.
Cover photograph by Michael Gilbert.
Cover design by Dik Campbell.
Book design by Shelley Sopher.
Typeset by Val Jakubowski.
Printed and bound in Canada.

Short excerpts have been quoted with gracious permission of the publishers: in "June's Night" page 45 quoted from "Stand by Your Man" by Tammy Wynette (CBS Records); in "June's Night" page 46 quoted from "A Good-Hearted Woman" by Waylon Jennings and Willie Nelson (RCA Victor); in "Levels of Existence" page 67 quoted from *The Prophet* by Kahlil Gibran, Toronto: Random House, 1982, p.36; in "Levels of Existence" page 71 quoted from "The Way Back into the Ground of Metaphysics" by Martin Heidegger in *Existentialism from Dostoevsky to Sartre* edited by Walter Kaufmann, New York: New American Library, 1975; in "Putting Things Away" page 82 quoted from *Where the Wild Things Are* by Maurice Sendak, New York: Harper & Row, 1963; and in "Life Skills" page 89 quoted from *The Prophet* by Kahlil Gibran, Toronto: Random House, 1982, p.16.

The author wishes to thank the members of the Bombay Bicycle Club for their critical judgement and support; Edna Alford for her editorial advice; and the Saskatchewan Arts Board for grants permitting her to work on some of these stories.

The publisher gratefully acknowledges the financial assistance of the City of Regina, the Saskatchewan Arts Board, the Canada Council, and the Department of Communications.

Canadian Cataloguing in Publication Data
Wesseler, Marlis, 1952-
    Life skills
    (McCourt fiction series ; 7)
    ISBN 1-55050-040-6
I. Title. II. Series
PS8595.E77L5 1992   C813'.54   C92-098133-X
PR9199.3.W47L5 1992

COTEAU BOOKS
401 - 2206 Dewdney Avenue
Regina, Saskatchewan
Canada S4R 1H3

Dedicated to the memory of my parents

Contents

1
The Wall

7
Whale Watching

16
Northern Lights

25
The Gift

30
Marx on the Wall

36
Bliss Symbols

44
June's Night

49
Border Lines

55
The Inheritance

61
Indecent Exposure

65
Levels of Existence

75
Putting Things Away

83
Life Skills

The Wall

BARBARA AND HANS WALKED THROUGH THE ANCIENT ARCHWAY leading from the bar to the cobblestone street. They strolled along various sidestreets until they came to Königstrasse. Barbara felt glamorous and European, like Marlene Dietrich or Greta Garbo, and wished she could see Berlin the way it had been before the war, before everything old was bombed. She wanted to see real cabarets; she wanted to dance in the Grand Hotel. She looked down at the supple leather of her high-heeled boots, pleased at how she, with her narrow feet, had no trouble finding boots here that fit perfectly.

She stopped. Brown mush was oozing out from under the heel of her left boot. Self-satisfied Berliners hurried around her, none of them noticing anything on their own boots. Why did things like this always happen to her?

Hans looked at her and grinned his good-naturedly evil smile. That was why she had married him, she thought sometimes, because of his smile. She scraped her boots on the sidewalk in disgust. "Berlin must be the dog shit capital of the world. It's unbelievable."

"My grandmother says Paris is vorse," Hans said, lazily leaning against a *currywurst* stand.

The first time Barbara met Hans's family, they had all gathered together to meet her. There were hearty handshakes and laughter and enthusiastic guttural speech accompanied by touches to kneecaps, wrists, shoulders; Barbara found it exhausting and bewildering. The grandmother had sat ignoring everyone, gazing silently at her own thoughts, and finally Barbara sat down on the couch beside her and made hesitant conversation: two quiet foreigners in exuberant territory.

The old woman reminisced about her girlhood, conjuring up stories of dances and fairy tale evenings of frosted drinks at summer spas, *glühwein* around the fireplace at winter resorts in the Alps. When she was a girl her hair was so long, she said, she could sit on it. She used to play the piano at friends' houses, her back straight, as she had been taught, white hands held delicately above the keys, wrists flexible and dainty, her long chocolate brown hair almost touching the carpet. She remembered herself in a white dress with a red sash, with a red ribbon in her hair. "Ach, but now I am an old woman," she had said to Barbara, and she patted her hand and smiled.

They continued their walk, Barbara watching the sidewalk until she realized where they were. There it was again. They kept running into it. A perfectly normal street, pavement over cobblestone, would suddenly lead to thick cement looming over them, a dead end. Wooden-faced soldiers watching, at attention on top of tall stands that resembled lifeguard towers. Death guards, she'd thought, on first seeing them. Most sections of the wall were dirty cement grey covered with sprayed graffiti, fluorescent greens or oranges looking like Phentex yarn strewn over a basement floor. In the no-man's land between east and west was the odd Doberman or German shepherd, which could only be seen from tourist stands or hills overlooking the wall.

She had gone sightseeing with Hans's relatives, and each time, the wall was pointed out to her: "*Da. Da ist die Mauer.*" It was said with a certain pride, she thought, intermingled with a satisfied sense of communal self-pity. Berliners had long ceased to feel horror or sorrow whenever they passed the wall, simply because it had been there so long; it had become ordinary. It was an inconvenience that couldn't be helped, rather like bad weather. In fact, she realized, Berliners pointed out the wall in much the same way people from Saskatchewan spoke about their winters.

"Sometimes it's forty below," she'd found herself saying to one of Hans's friends.

"*Mein Gott, das ist wie in Siberien!*" he exclaimed, and she'd nodded smugly, pleased.

"There's ze wall," Hans said.

"I know," she said abruptly. "Let's get out of here for awhile, let's take a drive to the forest." There were islands of parkland in and surrounding Berlin, part of the city's property. After a twenty-minute drive, they left the car near the woods and started to walk, shuffling through the thick mat of fallen leaves.

"Forest." Barbara looked around at the ancient oak trees, brown-gold carpet, vines out of Grimm's fairy tales. "We don't even use that word at home, we say 'bush.' " They stopped beside a huge oak tree that was split almost in two. "How on earth did that happen? Lightning? I think it's still alive, look at the colour of the wood."

"Zat," Hans said, looking seriously at her with wide grey eyes, "is the famous Berliner Baumgartnerschnitzenschmatzen, one of the great vonders of the world. It's been like that for five hundred years and was a great tourist attraction even then. Why, I remember coming here as a youngster . . . " He started his atrocious imitation of an American accent and Barbara poked him.

"Great vonders of ze vorld," she imitated. "You're really too much." They began to wrestle. Hans chased her around vine-covered trees, huge, centuries old, the bark rough and friendly beneath their hands. He caught her and they fell together onto the soft golden carpet, but got up immediately when they discovered the mushy underlay of rotted vegetation.

They started to walk again, arm in arm. "I expect to find a house made of gingerbread any minute now," Barbara said.

There it was again. They stopped. The wall seemed to loom larger, more incongruous in the deserted forest, as if it were a giant prop for a science fiction movie.

"White," she said. "Only the Germans would bother to whitewash something like the wall. Can you believe it?"

Hans shrugged and walked to higher ground, where he could see over the wall into no-man's land. "Come here," he shouted, "look at these dogs."

She ran to him and saw two Doberman pinschers racing silently along the inside of the wall, ears razor flat, intent, swiftly becoming small dots in the distance, closing in on another somewhat taller dot.

Barbara's stomach knotted; she felt as if someone had touched her spine with something cold and sharp. "Did you hear a shot?"

"I'm not sure."

They watched. The dots were like those in a video game: search and destroy. The two finally descended on the one, the one disappearing, all three becoming one mass, a larger dot. Finally more dots appeared.

"Let's go." Hans's face was white. Barbara continued to stare, unable to move her legs. "Let's go!" he shouted and grabbed her arm. They ran through the decaying leaves, dodging gigantic tree trunks with bare witch-armed branches, tripping on vines, feathered branches from juniper trees brushing their faces.

"Do you think," she said, breaking the silence on the drive back, "do you think they were chasing some *guy*? Someone trying to get to West Berlin?"

"No, it was probably an exercise, zey were training the dogs."

"But . . ."

"Ya, it was only a training exercise."

She wondered if the soldiers were Russians or East Germans. Likely they were Russian; surely they couldn't count on an East German to shoot. "Have they ever posted East German soldiers on the wall?" she asked.

"They're all East German," Hans said in careful English. "All the guards."

She looked at him and said nothing. It had likely been a training exercise.

They spent the rest of the day quietly reading and writing breezy, everything's fine postcards. That evening they went to a movie, an American comedy with German subtitles. Barbara's laughter became almost spontaneous by the last half of the show.

The next day they went to the zoo. At least we can't run into the wall here, she thought, watching an elephant scratch himself against the cement of his enclosure. Clean striped tigers, looking artificial, somehow, paced back and forth in their cage. "Let's go and see the monkeys," she said. "They're all inside."

The primates were behind glass rather than bars, so a person could walk right up and stand nose to nose with any of them. The faces were what interested her: the shrivelled yet babyish chimps; the flat-faced, reserved baboons; the enthusiastic, bearded orangutan; the great variety of chittering, surprised-looking monkeys.

The walls of each cage had loops and ladders of rope attached to them; a variety of apes and monkeys clambered from the walls to the floors and back again, fighting, screeching, playing, each species housed in a separate cage. The orangutan and chimpanzees made a game of putting sacks over their heads and snatching them off again, much to the amusement of the onlookers. A few, however, refused to play. They put the sacks over their heads and sat like lumpy potato bags in corners, or swung like hanging lampshades from the walls. A giant ape suddenly squatted and put his hand under himself.

"Good God, he's catching his own shit in his hand," Barbara said.

A dark man standing beside them smiled, his gold fillings catching the light. "Ya," he said, "he used to amuse himself by throwing his *dreck* at the people, when these were cages with bars."

The ape had a calculating, sly expression. He pretended to be about to throw, waiting for a reaction from the people he was observing. The reaction, instead of the mass panic he seemed to expect, was one of condescending amusement. He looked perplexed, faked a throw once or twice and finally, there it was, splattered on the glass in front of Barbara.

"What else?" she said. The ape looked bewildered.

Hans nudged her. "Vat's that saying about people in glass houses?"

The ape swung unsteadily across the cage to the glass. He stood swaying back and forth, gazing stupidly, eyes rolling: a crazy metronome.

"Something's wrong with him," Barbara said softly, uncomfortable. The ape continued to rock from side to side until, with concentrated fury, he attacked the glass, kicking it, making it ring loud hollow bongs, punching it until he sat, exhausted, on the floor. He began his insane cradle rock rhythm again, and Hans and Barbara walked out.

It was beginning to rain when they left the zoo; the sidestreets were grey and shiny under the *Kneiper* signs. "We have to be at your grandmother's by six-thirty," she said, as they got into his father's tiny Fiat.

Hans's grandmother rented an apartment in a modern building where other elderly people lived, and managed to keep her beige carpet, the flowered couch, the china cabinet and all the other furniture and knick-knacks spotless. Barbara remembered, when she first met her at the family get-together, noticing her skin. She had the smoothest skin Barbara had ever seen on someone so old. Not that she looked young, it was just that her face hadn't wrinkled. It was round and smooth, with slightly sagging cheeks and a few broken veins creating faint blotches.

She greeted them at the door with energy and enthusiasm and fed them a huge supper. After dessert, she sat down comfortably with her brandy and started reminiscing. Hans's parents never discussed the war seriously, although his mother had once said, about the concentration camps with their high walls and barbed wire, "We didn't know what went on; we had no idea," and Barbara believed her. But late in the evening Hans's grandmother spoke in slow direct German, looking straight at Barbara. "When I was a girl we were a rich family. Then came the depression and the inflation and we were ruined by Jewish speculators. Others as well as us. By Jews. Jews were not popular, we called them pigs. Then Hitler came and they all disappeared."

Barbara felt the ice on her spine again, the same as she'd felt watching the "training exercise." She watched Hans's expression change from that of shock to apology (she's only an old lady) to belligerence (she's here and she's my grandmother, whether it suits you or not). He stood up and thanked the old woman for supper and said they had to get back. She nodded, looking closely at Barbara's face before she kissed her goodbye. Hans, Barbara realized, had inherited his smile from his grandmother.

"Most of us say we didn't know what was happening back then," she said, "but we knew enough. We knew what to turn our backs to."

On the way to his parents' apartment, Hans said, "She's had a hard life. Her parents lost everysing and died in poverty when she was young and the Russians killed her husband in a work camp after the war. Then she lost her house in East Germany. She calls the Russians pigs too."

"And that's supposed to make everything fine? That she calls the Russians pigs *too?*"

They drove on in silence for awhile, then Barbara asked, "Did I understand everything? Did—"

"Remember, she's eighty years old," he interrupted. "Who knows what goes on in her mind. Anyway I didn't hear all she said." His voice was harsh and resentful, against her, Barbara realized, not his grandmother.

She leaned her head back on the headrest and closed her eyes. They hadn't talked about the incident at the wall, and now they weren't going to talk about this. Fine, she thought, this is the end of it. A newscaster on the car radio was speaking German too quickly for her to follow. She wanted to go home. She wanted to be able to turn on the radio and hear Peter Gzowski's mellow but earnestly Canadian voice. Thinking of that voice made her want to cry. She glanced at Hans's grim face and reached over and touched his knee. This is only a holiday, she thought, in a few days we'll leave it all behind.

Whale Watching

CALL ME ISABEL. MY FATHER, MAY HE REST IN PEACE, WAS THE ONLY one who dared call me Izzy, and I have not heard the name mentioned in my presence since his death. I was greatly saddened by his passing, as they say, but I still sometimes feel a guilty relief when I remember I will never have to put up with that name again.

My father, who was fond of puns, would have been amused by my misquoting Herman Melville in my own narrative. I remember him reading *Moby Dick*, *Call of the Wild*, *King Solomon's Mines*, and various Zane Grey series. I read them all too, taking the sexism and racism for granted as part of the adventures. I have inherited his books and now, when I read excerpts from any of them, I am amazed at the sheer extent of the paternalism, all the talk about spirited women and horses; and savages, noble and ignoble. Yet I still feel a fascination with these books and vividly remember details of characters, especially Captain Ahab, swivelling on his whalebone leg pegged into a hollow on the deck of the *Pequod*, intent in his search for his white demon, the savage harpooneers and all the rest of the crew hypnotized into making Moby Dick their own quest.

They are good books in spite of everything and I would like to pass them on to a child of my own, even though I know real children nowadays are more interested in *Star Wars* and computers.

Although my father gave the impression of being an easy-going man, he had the stern sense of duty and self-importance of a Victorian gentleman constantly dealing with inferiors. He was always scrupulously polite, and could manipulate in a teasing, charming way those who couldn't be influenced directly. I learned how to read him when I was very young, and so he considered me to be a prodigy. I honestly believe I was one of the only people for whom he had any respect. Certainly my mother never received her share, from him or from me, and has had to rely on my cousins for solace and comfort in her old age.

I come to Victoria to see my mother about once a year, usually at

Christmas. This year I decided to get my visit over with during summer vacation so I could go somewhere warm and exotic for Christmas holidays. As it turned out, she began to drive me to drink shortly after I arrived at her apartment, so I decided to take a few days off, and have come here to the west coast of Vancouver Island.

At this point in time, as I say in the memos I write in my office, I am staying in a pleasant, picturesque village inhabited by tourists and superannuated hippies. The people in the tourist office are friendly and helpful, and the girl who recommended I take the whale watching tour said there are whales summering here, and she could guarantee I'd see at least one.

I'm not the type of person who seeks adventure, but a boat ride on a sunny evening in July seemed to be a pleasant idea. Besides, ever since I read *Moby Dick* I've had a certain interest in whales, and thought I would like to see one in its natural habitat.

I knew enough about boating to wear a warm jacket and something to cover my ears, but when I reached the boat dock this evening, I was given a rubber outfit that looked like a cross between a parka and overalls. Instead of questioning the type of ride which would produce a need for such protective clothing I, along with seven other rather meek-looking individuals, struggled into our suits and made our way over to where the tour boat was supposed to be. The organizer, a woman who, in a former life, must have been a kindergarten teacher, herded us all to the end of the dock, beside which bobbed a rubber dinghy. A Zodiac, it was called. It's practically untippable, she said.

Now, here I must plead profound ignorance. I had never been out in any body of water larger than Nesslin Lake in northern Saskatchewan and had not the faintest idea what the open Pacific would be like. It seemed to be a calm evening, and besides, a sense of lethargy came over me as soon as I saw the boat. Whatever happened, happened; this was meant to be, and I'd already paid my twenty-five dollars.

The other tourists were couples, soft-stomached businessmen and their wives, and one child, who sat with his parents in front of the driver. The seats were plastic milk crates covered with particle board. Since life jackets didn't seem to be considered necessary, and since they probably wouldn't fit over our overalls anyway, we sat on them. The water lapped gently against the rubber sides of the boat. The sky was cloudless and benign.

The men joked about the possibility of literally running into a whale, and the father of the boy said to him, "Wish hard for a whale," as if it were something he might get for Christmas. He was maybe five years old, and sometimes children that age, snuggled against their mothers on buses or at fairs or picnics at the end of a day, give me an almost physical sense of longing and loss. If I had taken my last chance to get pregnant, I might have a child like that now. Perhaps I would have sat in the back of the boat with my child leaning against my knee, anticipating adventure. But how would I be managing, really, with a small child? I'm impatient and set in my ways, I like order and peace and quiet and am intolerant of silliness. I would not be a good mother. Still, I have always thought of birth as being somehow miraculous.

The driver of the boat was lean in the way of outdoor types who have hardened with age. His face looked stretched and lined, a couple of his teeth were missing and his cheekbones seemed ready to break through his skin. He considered us to be a group of sheep, but kept his disdain fairly well hidden.

We started off, the small boat giving us a bumpy but tolerable ride through the sheltered inlet. I thought this wasn't going to be bad at all, and looked forward to seeing whales. I was glad I'd brought my sunglasses; the sun was beginning to sink into the horizon and shone directly on our faces. We ploughed our way blindly through the choppy waves, vaguely aware of the green coast and the smell of salt water and seaweed. The sea, the wind blowing through my hair, the evening sun, everything contributed to a feeling of mild elation that I thought might lead to exhilaration if we actually saw any whales.

Soon, however, we hit open water, where some of the waves were at least five feet high. This may not seem awe-inspiring to someone raised near the ocean, but I am from the prairies. Our guide turned his Zodiac directly into the waves and proceeded to drive full throttle, forcing the boat to crash with bone jarring violence from one wave to another. I ceased to feel elated and hung on for dear life, one hand on the rope beside me and one on the belt of the man in front of me. At this point I did not care whether that would be considered socially acceptable or not. We slammed into wave after wave, mile after mile. I would recover from one crash only to have to tense my stomach and eventually my entire body for the next one. I made up my mind. This was going to be an ordeal that would have to be endured, and I entered a kind of dazed condition in which suffering was the order of the day and all that could be done was to wait it out. It didn't occur to me to ask the driver to stop; my headache, backache and bruises had become, in my mind, inevitable; the ride was timeless and spaceless and I had no control. I felt nothing would be done even if I screamed, even if I stood up. I was nothing, I was totally powerless and had to remain passive because the ride was all; it was The Ride and nothing else existed and I could only hope that sometime it might end.

Now, suffering with a group is one thing, and suffering alone is another. But being the only one suffering in a group is truly awful. I was attempting not to think of what I had eaten for dinner when it suddenly permeated my consciousness that the others were enjoying themselves. Or rather, they were letting on that they were enjoying themselves, which was worse, because they were being good sports and I wasn't. The man in front of me whooped like a cowboy every time we hit a particularly huge wave. The man across from me made comments like, "Man the lifeboats me hearties," and the father, sitting next to the boy, said "Whee!" immediately after the cowboy-businessman whooped. What's more, the wives, uncomfortable as they were, contributed to the good cheer by smiling indulgently. Worse than Americans, I thought. There is nothing more obnoxious than a group of Canadian tourists. We could be entering the jaws of hell and some idiot would make a good-humoured remark about the change in the weather.

The boat stopped, and bobbed like a cork for awhile as we gazed at each other through our water-spattered glasses. We were all soaked. The driver said it was a bit rougher than usual though still perfectly safe, and wondered if anybody would like to go back. This brought complete silence as each of us pondered the prospect of being the spoilsport. I should have said something, of course, but I too have been indoctrinated with the spirit of good sportsmanship which, even though pioneering is dead, seems to be instilled in the unconscious of every Canadian. Whatever you feel, don't ruin it for anyone else. There are always the exceptions that prove the rule, such as my Aunt Janet. She could be counted on to complain loudly about the slightest inconvenience and ruin the day for anyone within hearing distance. Accordingly, she became a family joke, and any complaining or whining in our house was called "creating a Janet." To this day, I can never complain about a meal to the waiter or ask someone at work not to smoke in my office without hearing my father say, "Creating a Janet again eh, Izzy?" She was, naturally, my mother's sister.

Finally the cowboy asked how far we were from the whales, and the guide said we were well over halfway there. Of course then everyone said why not go on, which was exactly what he was counting on. I began to hate him with the kind of impersonal hatred one may have for a force beyond anyone's power, like a tornado or earthquake, or the ocean itself.

We continued the tour. By this time I was beginning to feel nauseated, or "nauseous" as my secretary would say, with so much veracity that I have never bothered to correct her. In fact, during her pregnancy she was nauseous so often that I considered letting her go, as they say. The term "fired" is not in current use in our department. One's position is defunct, one is terminated, one's contract is not renewed, one's mandate has been fulfilled, one is laid off, one's position has become redundant. I have even heard it said that someone had been dehired. I am beginning to wonder if, even after fifteen years, someone on high will find *my* position to be redundant.

My secretary never worries about being unemployed. She is versatile, she says, and could work at anything: waitress, daycare worker, grass cutter for city parks. In fact she has done all of these and more. She doesn't worry if things go wrong at the office, she simply manages the best she can and if her supervisors don't like it they can lump it. She drives me to the edge of insanity every time I see her filing her nails or chatting with her friends, and she irritates me beyond belief even when she's doing her work.

I have tried over the years to be tolerant with her. I have blamed myself and thought my dislike may be simple jealousy. She is twenty-nine and pretty. She had the courage to purposely become pregnant without being married. She has had many affairs, including one with Richard, our office's eligible bachelor, whom I once considered going out with until she told me his nickname among the secretaries is Mobile Dick. She tells jokes to her male superiors and flirts shamelessly, yet manages to be well-liked by the other women in the office. She wears white well.

All of the above are traits which I have, at one time or another, envied. However, many other women have qualities which I wish I had and I do not dislike them. I have tried to decide exactly what it is about her that bothers me so much, but always end up running into a white wall in my mind. I simply dislike her and it is our misfortune that we have to work together.

The boat finally slowed and we found ourselves at the whale grounds. By this time I was sick, and the change from slamming into waves to bobbing and rolling with them produced the anticipated effect. I hung over the side while everyone else politely looked away, admired the view and wished for whales. I was rinsing my mouth with salt water when the first leviathan, as Herman Melville would say, was sighted.

The whooping businessman stood up in the boat and tried to take a photograph, fumbling with his camera, first peeling it out of a plastic bag. This final piece of idiocy was only what I had expected but still, even in my misery, I was about to say, "Do you want to kill us all?" when the driver asked him to sit down. I realized at this point that I hadn't said one word to anyone since the tour began.

The other tourists, true to form, seemed to be quite excited about the slimy grey lump that had briefly shown itself to us, and were eager to see more. I thought now that we'd seen one, we might just as well begin the gruelling journey home, but no, we were committed to touring the bay. We spotted another one. This time Buffalo Bill managed to take a picture, although I imagine his friends won't be overly impressed with a blurry shot of a blob protruding from a wave.

After awhile, more and more grey spotted backs were seen diving placidly in and out of the water, and the entire boatload of tourists were beside themselves, including me. I thought, if I live through this I will never go anywhere again as long as I live. I prayed. Please, I said to somebody omnipotent, please get me out of this. I remember my father saying once (or rather he thought he had said it only once) that there are no atheists in a foxhole. That may well apply to situations other than war.

Since the sun was no longer shining in my face I decided to change my sunglasses for my regular glasses, which were zip-locked into a pocket on my leg. I should have worn my contact lenses, but am no longer in the habit of wearing them. I noticed, one day, that glasses cover some of the crowsfeet around my eyes so that I look younger with them on.

I have never been sure of my looks. Even when I was young I didn't know whether I was really attractive or not. I remember going out for dinner with a group of my co-workers and enjoying myself, laughing and talking and being quite vivacious, as far as my social capabilities allowed. I felt, rather than saw, the new middle manager of our section staring at me, and I thought maybe there were some possibilities here. The evening went by, I knew he was sneaking looks at me, I felt relaxed and expansive and didn't need to use the washroom until I got home, where I noticed a tiny gob hanging from a nose hair, lodged just securely enough to appear and disappear with each breath. It could be quite hypnotic, I thought, as I watched it blow in and out. I realized that the people I knew well at the table might have told me if I'd had a piece of lettuce between my teeth, or a smudge of mustard on my lip, but nobody would have been prepared to say, "You have a piece of dried snot hanging from your nose."

After that kind of experience I cringe every time I think of it for a day or two and then regain some kind of perspective. Who knows if anyone noticed? Who cares? But basically, I do. I want to be sought after and desired, I want to be beautiful but dignified, elegant with a hint of passion lurking behind the mystery of my eyes. The knowledge that I've passed my prime without ever realizing I was experiencing it fills me with a melancholy that almost rivals my periods of regret at having no children.

My mother has never overcome the somewhat quaint notion that it is her duty to find me a husband. She is not East European, so I have no idea where she acquired the art of matchmaking, an art which, in my case, has had a singular lack of success. Sometimes I think the main reason I have never married is to spite my mother. And of course, I am an only child, and the lack of grandchildren drives her mad. I wonder what her reaction to an illegitimate baby would have been? In the end, I think, where other women would have become doting grandmothers in spite of the child's parentage, my mother would have been overcome more with shame than with joy and could not have coped with both me and her friends at the same time. She could not exist without her bridge-playing group, and so we would have been disowned, which might have worked out best for all concerned. Sometimes I wonder why I have the capacity to go on and on like this about situations that don't exist. Furthermore, how can I be concerned about not having a child when my relationship with my own mother is so disastrous?

The boat continued to rock as I changed into clear glasses. Unfortunately they soon became as wet as the sunglasses, so my vision did not noticeably improve.

"The grey whale," the driver was saying, "weighs up to sixty tons and can be as long as fifty feet."

It dawned on me, meanwhile, that the reason no one was too concerned about wearing life jackets was because the water was so cold we'd die of exposure before we had a chance to drown. A whale showed itself and blew its spout a few yards away and, amid the exclamations of the others, I began, now that I was no longer so sick, to feel distinctly nervous. Considering that the part of each whale we could see was only the tip of the proverbial iceberg, those that were close to us likely had a considerable part of their anatomies located directly underneath our boat. What's more, they seemed to be curious about us, seedy little group that we were, and continued to call their friends and relatives over for a closer look. We were in a pod, our guide informed us, and I agreed, thinking that this stupid kayak or whatever it was called was about as safe as a pea pod, until I realized he meant the group of whales. They were all around us, some diving, leaving final glimpses of their horizontal tail fins, some suddenly emerging and blowing off spouts, sounding like giant kids puffing the last of their milkshakes through plastic straws.

"What kind of whale was Moby Dick?" asked the man across from me.

When our guide didn't hear him, I yelled, "Sperm."
"What?" he said.
"A sperm whale. Moby Dick was a sperm whale."

The other tourists looked at me surreptitiously, wondering if I was in any danger of again losing, as they say, my cookies, or whether, now that I had spoken, I would lighten up and become one of them. I sat quietly and waited for the boat to start moving.

My wet glasses were becoming aggravating so I reached into another pocket of my overalls and extracted a soggy Kleenex. As I proceeded to smear water from one side of each lens to the other, our guide yelled and pointed past the front of the boat, and everyone exclaimed in unison. I peered like a waterlogged Mr. McGoo into the distance but couldn't see clearly past the back of the man in front of me. I put on my glasses but they made my vision worse, if anything. I missed something that one is lucky, the guide said, to see once in a lifetime. A whale had breached, he said. It took a few minutes of deciphering the excited comments of the other tourists before I realized that when a whale "breaches" he comes straight up head first out of the water, giving the watcher a full view of the entire head and part of the body.

Well, I thought, surely after a climax such as this everyone will be ready to go home. The little boy had been very good the entire time. He dutifully became excited whenever he saw a whale, his wide eyes looking as often at his parents as at the giant sea mammals. Now he was falling asleep, reacting to the sun and fresh air, and the rocking motion of the boat.

Finally we started off. The return trip was not quite so intolerable because the driver, for some reason, developed the decency to slow down before we hit the bigger waves. It made a great difference. We rolled over the waves rather than smashing into them, and instead of appreciating his thoughtfulness I worked myself up into a rage wondering why he hadn't driven this way in the first place. I was so angry by the time we reached the dock that I didn't dare say anything. I am not one to make scenes. I silently took off my rubber overalls, put them down carefully on the dock, nodded at everyone in what I thought at the time was a polite manner, glared at the driver, and staggered rather than stalked (as I would have wished) to the car.

Now I am back in my hotel, which is a weathered collection of rooms overlooking the harbour, writing this instead of the indignant letter to the tourist office that was intended. Perhaps I will send it with a letter to a friend, but likely I'll keep it as a reminder, of what I'm not certain. Maybe of the fact that the sea and its mysteries no longer interest me, that my own white whale is beginning to swim off into the distance, and that I am no longer in a position to launch any kind of pursuit.

♦

Northern Lights

♦

THE NORTH WAS COMING OUT OF HIBERNATION; IT WAS BEGINNING to revive for the spring. Jill caught the wood-smoke, pine-tree and lake smell as she walked to the store, the warmth of the sun touching her head, making her feel blessed. A truck passed, and she heard her name called; someone leaned out of the window and waved. Jill waved back and opened the battered door of the general store.

"Did you hear the news?" Mac's voice startled her as she was separating an ancient shopping cart from its companions. Mac was the store manager, a delicately-built man with the movements and fastidious manner of a cat. He said he moved so quietly because of his years of hunting and trapping in the bush with his father. Jill thought he simply liked to disconcert people.

His real name was Larry Montpellier; he was a Cree Indian from The Pas, Manitoba. During his first year in Caribou Point he had renovated the store and insisted that his staff show up for work on time. He had also formed friendships with some of the whites. The local Dené Indians said he was an apple: red on the outside and white on the inside, and henceforth he was known as Mac, short for McIntosh. His girlfriends, he said, called him Delicious.

Jill dropped a couple of boxes of cereal in her cart before she replied. "What news?" she asked.

"Jesus is here," Mac said.

"Was it Methodius again?" Jill rolled her eyes, exaggerating her indifference.

Last fall, soon after Jill arrived to teach the adult upgrading class, Methodius Dauphin, a gangly twelve-year-old with an old-fashioned brushcut, said he had a vision. Apparently he saw Jesus at the pilgrimage grounds, beside the plaster statue of the Blessed Virgin, smiling benevolently. He returned home to tell his parents, who were drinking and playing poker with Prosper Big Eye and Jake Lamontaigne. Once there, however, he couldn't speak. A voice, he said later, told him to denounce his parents and their wicked ways and he became too frightened to say anything. Instead, he went into the living-room and had a fit.

Methodius told some of his schoolmates what had happened, and one evening toward twilight he went into another trance. They all claimed they saw a strange light glowing around him. This time he saw Jesus standing outside the pool hall listening to the jukebox play k.d. lang. Then he had another fit.

His friends were impressed. Within an hour the entire village had heard about his vision. Modeste Janvier, one of the band councillors, got together with Flannery Melnychuk, the principal of the school.

Modeste, a sloppy-looking man with stringy hair sticking out from under a perpetual baseball cap, had learned how to speak white English fifteen years earlier, while spending two years in jail for rape. He had returned to the reserve an efficient organizer with the rare ability to wheel and deal with government bureaucrats.

Flannery, the principal, was a tall man with dyed black hair and something of a hunted look. He had dyed his hair and grown a beard three years before, when he had been called for jury duty and hadn't wanted to be recognized by the defendant or his family, in case he was convicted and they wanted revenge. As it turned out, Flannery was not chosen to be a juror, but the beard remained and his hair was still black, three years later.

Modeste and Flannery had cancelled school and called a meeting in the gym. The entire community turned out. Each boy who had been with Methodius when he saw Jesus was called up to the microphone to testify. They were near hysterics by the end of the day. It all seemed to fall so remarkably into place: Methodius was born on December 25th; twelve boys were with him when he lit up and went into a trance, if you counted Joe Dadzené's little brother; and wasn't his grandmother on his father's side named Mary?

The next day, the priest's arrival put an end to it all. He was a small man with light, nervous movements and a frail physique, so his deep voice always surprised new members of the congregation. He called a special Saturday service at the church.

His voice thundered down from the pulpit, striking shame into the people who had believed Methodius, and a feeling of righteousness into the people who had not. Flannery and Modeste, their enthusiasm considerably dampened, said afterwards that they hadn't believed, either, they just thought the boy needed help and attention.

He certainly had received attention, Jill thought. However, he went quietly back to school on Monday and everyone forgot about the incident over the winter.

Mac grinned and ran his fingers through his hair. "Yep, Methodius saw Jesus again, only this time His Holiness was out walking on the lake."

"Big deal. The ice hasn't gone out yet. It could have been anybody."

"Methodius said whoever it was had a blue robe and sandals, and long hair."

Jill started toward the refrigerated section, looking for oranges or grapefruit. "I suppose any search for fresh produce would be, uh, fruitless?"

Mac pulled her hat over her eyes. "Get real here. I'm telling you some news with international, if not universal, significance and you're concerned about Vitamin C?"

"It was probably Solomon Dadzené out on a spree. I know he's got blue sheets because his wife always has them hanging out on the clothesline. They're pretty holey too."

He shook his head in mock sorrow and began to repair a pyramid of Kraft dinners. Jill finished shopping, picked up her mail and climbed the easy slope to the top of White Hill, where the Indian Affairs trailers and houses huddled together like the shoebox mice the grade one kids had made in art.

She had to kick at her porch door to get it open; with the warm weather, everything in her trailer was becoming damp, and doors and windows were sticking shut. She unpacked the groceries and, feeling more energetic than usual, thought about cleaning up a bit. She noticed with some disgust that near the fridge and stove the raised flower images on the kitchen linoleum were outlined in dirt, and the green shag living-room carpet looked like grass in a well-used playground.

She decided instead to visit Monique, one of the students in her upgrading class, and find out all the gossip. Leaving her porch open, she walked through the village of multicoloured prefab houses until she came to a faded red and white bungalow. She knew Monique would know who was at the door, because only a white person would bother to knock and wait for an answer. Jill smiled, remembering the kids knocking on her front door last Halloween, shouting Trick or Treat. Almost every one of them, even the tiniest toddlers, had been dressed up as Mohawk Warriors.

Monique was a tall, big-boned woman of twenty-seven or so with a beautiful smile slightly marred by a chipped front tooth. She had two children but had refused to marry their father. She wanted kids, she said, but couldn't live with a man. She was strong-willed and tough and Jill admired her. Monique sensed this and calmly expected to get her grade ten certificate with no problem.

"Hi," she said. "Come on in. I've just put Owen to bed; him, he was awake all night with a cold. My mom, she's having a nap too. She doesn't sleep so well when the kids are sick."

"So," said Jill after a bit of small talk about the kids, "what's this about Methodius seeing Jesus again?"

"Oh that. Yeh he's at it again. Me, I went to see his mother this morning and there she was, praying. She thinks he's a saint the little bugger. She's joined AA this time."

"Methodius's mother? Well good for her, maybe now she can concentrate a bit on her kids instead of boozing it up all the time. Maybe Methodius finally got her attention."

"Hah." Monique looked vaguely amused.

Jill knew she was sounding like a middle-class schoolteacher. "Flannery isn't going to call off school this time, eh?"

Monique laughed. "Not that I heard. But there's going to be a prayer meeting at Dauphins' tonight and Methodius is going to lead."

The sun was beginning to set as Jill walked back to her trailer. She could hear dogs barking, kids shouting, skidoos buzzing over the melting snow, and a faint echo of music from the pool hall. She thought she'd go down with Lisa to Mac's later on and watch movies on the Bay's video machine and drink rye. She hadn't noticed any signs of life in Lisa's trailer, but thought maybe she was taking a nap. This year's grade one class wasn't an easy bunch to handle.

Lisa was from Nova Scotia, but had been in Caribou Point now for two years. She was slight, pretty and blond. Jill's students said they often gave Indian nicknames to the whites who came to work in their village; the school superintendent, for example, who would fly in for a few hours and fly out again, never staying overnight, was called something which meant "big white day bird." Lisa's Indian name, however, was "Barbie Doll." Jill asked what her own nickname was, and they wouldn't tell her. They said she didn't have one yet.

Lisa lived in the trailer next to Jill's and they'd become friends partly from simple necessity. They didn't have much in common except both were white and single, and both were teachers. They did like some of the same kinds of music, and often got together after school to have a drink and listen to Waylon Jennings, The Judds, or old Patsy Cline albums. Once in a blue moon one of them would help the other clean house. They'd put on a Stan Rogers tape and spend part of an afternoon drinking Southern Comfort, mopping floors and belting out "Northwest Passage" or "Barrette's Privateers."

    Jill's contracts took her to a different community every year. They lasted anywhere from five to eight months and left her free to travel the rest of the time. She had started teaching adult upgrading in her late twenties, intending to work for a year or two and then find a job in the city. Somehow, though, she never got around to looking for one. She liked the North and the independence it offered, and she realized after a few years that she like being a nomad. She kept her few possessions at her parents' place in the summers, and they had given up on her settling down. She'd been married for a year once, when she was just out of university. That was enough, she always said, to last her a lifetime.

    She was easy-going up to a point and could live with anyone, she thought, for half a year or so, which was a good thing because she often had to stay with teachers from the regular school system who had housing provided for them. Sometimes her college managed to negotiate an empty Indian Affairs trailer or an apartment in a nursing station and she was able to have a place to herself. She'd spent one winter in a cabin advertised in tourist brochures as "rustic," and one year she'd done a six-month contract living in an empty office beside the classroom. Her rent, however, was often next to nothing, and she lived simply, able to save her money for trips to Europe or the States in the summertime. She decided that when she reached forty she would quit travelling and save money to invest in a house somewhere. She had three years left to go.

    Jill walked up the road leading to her trailer, contemplating the Bay's selection of videotapes which included such all-time greats as *Friday the Thirteenth Part Ten*, *High Road to China*, *What the Swedish Butler Saw*, and *Texas Chainsaw Massacre II*. She considered staying home that evening and reading; all the other teachers had gone south for the weekend. Finally she remembered *High Road to China* starred Tom Selleck and she decided to go to Mac's. No matter how pitiful the actual movie was, there was a chance that Tom Selleck might take his shirt off.

    She'd just started to make some hamburgers when Lisa phoned. She was already at Mac's and he was cooking a roast and why didn't Jill come on down for supper. Mac and Lisa had some kind of thing going, but Jill wasn't sure what, exactly. Lisa always made sure that Jill was along, or expected to come along any minute, and then she'd sit beside Mac all evening, giving him the eye and touching his arm until Jill decided to go home. Then Lisa would jump up and come along with her. She could see that Mac found Lisa attractive, but he didn't seem to care about getting her into bed, maybe because, if Jill could believe her students' gossip, he already had a different girl for every day of the week. She didn't know whether Lisa had heard the gossip or was simply shy, or whether she was thinking twice because Mac was an Indian. Whatever, Jill thought, it was certainly none of her business.

Jill was older than both of them, and considered herself out of the running. Besides, she preferred not to become involved with men in the North. She had learned that when she did, she was, one way or another, stuck with them. Even if the guy was a one-night stand, even if she split up with him after a week or two, there he'd be, showing up at parties, standing behind her in the line-up for mail or walking by her front window every day until the end of her contract. It was even worse if she and the guy actually liked each other and they got to be known as a couple. Then she'd be expected to spend most of her free time in his company.

Mac's house was directly beside the store, an old clapboard structure with a red roof, built before the era of prefabs. Jill could hear the music from his stereo when she was halfway down the hill. When she got to the house, she could see that Mac and Lisa were already well into the rye. They greeted her with an obscene version of "Jack and Jill Went Up the Hill" which she had heard so often she could only groan.

"Come into the kitchen, Dzill, and eat. I'm starving." Mac lost his ability to pronounce certain consonant blends whenever he'd had a few drinks. This always made Jill slightly uncomfortable, because it reminded her of the few Cree Indians she had gone to school with. She remembered herself imitating them at home with her brothers: "Give me a bag of tseezies and five dzawbreakers," and her father saying, "Some of them are the nicest people you'd ever want to meet when they're sober."

"You know the funny thing about Indians?" Jill said. It was now much later in the evening. "The funny thing is they're always laughing at you somewhere behind their eyes." She was quite drunk. "Even you, Mac."

"Even me. Thanks a lot."

"You know what I mean?"

"Humour," he mocked. "The weapon of the oppressed."

"Exactly," said Jill, trying not to slur any of her words. "Sometimes I do the same thing when I'm with men."

"Well, so what am I, then," he said, still grinning, "an oppressor or an oppressee?"

Lisa looked disgusted. "You cancel each other out. The two of you add up to a big zero. Anyway, Jill, you laugh at the people here too. What about when Jesus came to Caribou Point? You thought that was the biggest hoot you'd ever heard of."

"I wasn't laughing at Indians, I was laughing at fundamentalist Christians. Besides, Flannery isn't an Indian."

"So? So that's okay is it. To laugh at Christians? To laugh at Flannery Melnychuk?"

"Well, Lisa," Mac put his arm around her. "You've got to laugh at somebody."

Lisa blushed. "No you don't," she said.

Mac looked down at her. "Well," he said gently, "maybe you don't."

Jill finished the last of her drink and looked somewhat blearily at Lisa. "I'm going home. You want to walk with me?"

Lisa studied her fingernails and shook her head. Jill, feeling a maudlin wave of benevolence, refrained from saying, "It's about time," and said goodnight.

It was past three in the morning and she could hear nothing but her footsteps in the snow. She loved it here at night, the silence, the smell of spring lingering even in the early morning frost. Only a month ago, when she had walked back with Lisa one night, it had been forty below. The cold was so intense it had seemed to give off a sound, a high metallic ring just out of hearing range, the silence broken only by the snapping of tree branches and the snow squeaking under their feet.

Jill looked up at the stars. Whole galaxies appeared to glitter out of the darkness. She saw Orion about to sink out of sight, his broad shoulders and sword retiring for the spring and summer, and she saw, closer to the horizon, the northern lights. They were just beginning; she hadn't noticed them at first, but now she saw they were becoming stronger, more pronounced every second, and they were not the usual white-gold haze, but were quickly becoming a dramatic display of colour. Shades of pink, green and yellow light curtained across the night sky like veils on a dancer, pulsating to hidden music.

Maybe there was such a thing as the music of the spheres, she thought. Maybe the lights were Salome's veils. Was that poetic or what. Jill tried to remember exactly how many rye-and-Sevens she'd drunk. She walked slowly, watching the northern lights become more spectacular. Salome, dancing with her seven veils all the colours in the prism, dancing to the music of the spheres, and only Jill perceptive enough to see the show. Salome dancing for Orion. Talk about mixing your myths. Jill imagined the seven veils filmy and irridescent, enveloping, then floating, creating an aura of mystic sensuality around a dark Salome, with Orion, one of his hands resting on the head of a lion (or was it just a big dog?), another on the hilt of his sword, standing frozen, watching.

Jill stopped. There was a form, a real person, standing in the middle of the road, near the pool hall. She hesitated, wondering whether to go back to Mac's or to keep walking. She was suddenly nervous about being alone; she thought about Modeste, the band councillor and ex-rapist. She realized the figure was too small to be Modeste so she went on. It was Methodius; he was in a trance, staring at the pool hall.

She decided to ignore him and go home, but then thought, what if he had a fit, keeled over and died of exposure? How would she feel if his body were found lying there in the morning? She called his name, her voice feeling hollow, seeming to echo. He didn't move. "Methodius!" She touched his shoulder, lightly tapping it, reminding herself ridiculously of an actor in an old movie: "Hey buddy can you spare a dime?" or "Excuse me, that's my goil yer dancin' wit." Sober up, she told herself. He still didn't move.

Jill felt a slight waver of panic. She could always go back and get Mac, she thought. Not that he and Lisa would appreciate the interruption. Oh God, what if she woke Methodius up and he had a fit? She didn't even have a broom handle or anything for him to bite on.

She started to turn back, then thought, Don't be stupid, go and get his mother. But what if they were drinking? She stopped and looked back at the boy. He started to move away in a halting sleepwalker's shuffle.

"Methodius!" she called. "Are you all right?" He turned toward her, not as a sleepwalker would, but with a sudden energy that made Jill flinch. She was ready to run.

He stood for a moment in silence, then raised both arms as if he were a performer accepting applause and said, "Fear not, I am the first and the last, and the living one; I died and behold I am alive forevermore, and I have the keys of Death and Hades. Now write what you see, what is and what is to take place hereafter. As for the mystery of the seven stars which you saw in my right hand, and the seven golden lampstands . . . "

He paused and stood uncertainly for a short while, listening, and then, just when Jill began to wonder if she should lead him home he began again, his voice this time losing its cracked adolescent quality and becoming almost as powerful as the priest's: "Behold, I am coming soon, bringing my recompense, to repay every one for what he has done. I am the Alpha and the Omega, the first and the last, the beginning and the end." He stopped and, again assuming the manner of a sleepwalker, started to move away. She followed him until she saw him open the door of his father's house.

Jill was shivering by the time she got home. She should make some tea and sober up, she thought, but instead sat down on the couch by the window. She sat there in the dark until morning, watching the stars disappear.

The Gift

THEY HAD BEEN WALKING FOR HOURS IN THE HOT SUN WITH THE Mediterranean on their right, sparkling far below the harsh faces of the cliffs. Kathleen was irritated and tired, but felt smug with the certainty that she had been right in the first place. Nobody with any sense would walk across an entire island to see a run-down monks' house.

The landscape was dry and sparse. Hills of rock jutted from barren land, ending in a sudden drop to the sea. It had been Allan's idea to see the monastery. All she wanted to do was lie on the beach, and since the day might end up being a failure and it would be his fault, he was angry with her. They had come to Amorgós partly because it was not a popular tourist spot. They were, Allan said, travellers rather than tourists.

Kathleen trailed farther and farther behind, acting more exhausted than she was, working herself up, exaggerating her thirst and the effect of the sun beating down on her head. She tried to hallucinate and almost succeeded in seeing a mirage of sand and cacti.

She watched Allan stalk farther down the path along the cliff, his shoulders set stubbornly as he disappeared around the curve of a hill. She was surprised when he reappeared and waited for her, then astonished when she moved close enough to see his expression. It had transformed from sullen stubborness to wonder and pleasure. She allowed herself to smile.

He took her hand and said, "Close your eyes, I have a gift for you." She closed her eyes; this was something Allan had done before, given her gifts. Once it had been early in the morning in Morocco. He came into the tent, woke her and said, "Come with me and don't open your eyes until I tell you." She had stumbled out of the tent, holding his arm, half awake, and when she opened her eyes she was in another, ancient world. Scarves of mist rose over a hillside village, miles away. The buildings, built of clay from the red earth, melted into the hills. Outlined against the village stood a single camel and its rider. While the sun rose, the silhouette became clearer and a voice came faintly through the still air chanting, in Arabic, a song or a prayer.

Another time they were on the beach in Israel and he had put his hand on her sun-warmed back and said, "I have a present for you. Sit up and look out past the pier. Look only there, nowhere else." She shut everything from her sight except the spot where he told her to look, and there they were: Tweedledum and Tweedledee. Identical twins about fifty years old were sitting, one on either side of an inner tube, each an exact reflection of the other: bald heads circled by brownish grey fringes, bellies like red beach balls forcing the inner tube under the water, round faces grinning gleefully. They floated around and around, moving slowly away from the crowd of swimmers, like hippo ballerinas in a cartoon.

Allan had a gift for presenting her with perfect scenes frozen in time, snapshots from another dimension. To him, each picture was whole, entire, beginning and ending with itself, and he presented the scenes to her with delight, as if they were jewels. They stayed in her memory, frozen images she could bring out and turn over again and again with pleasure.

But she remembered other things too. In Morocco that same morning they had seen a man driving a plough pulled by a woman. And in Israel, when the twins were lying in the sun on matching blankets, Kathleen noticed numbers tattooed on their wrists. She kept these images, too, as the undersides of Allan's gifts: they were part of the same material, never as clear or as beautiful, but certainly as valuable.

Now there was to be another gift. As they walked along the rough path she held his hand, her eyes closed, remembering a scene from an old movie. What was it? A woman meets her lover on the edge of a cliff and as she closes her eyes expecting a kiss he pushes her over the edge? Or did he only try and not succeed? Was she rescued by a hero who had loved her all along and kept an eye on her because he knew evil when he saw it?

"Open your eyes," Allan said, and her first impression was of something dazzling against shades of blue. The monastery was a stark white, whiter than any snow she could remember. Built to overhang the cliff, it seemed to have no connection with the earth, only with the sea and sky. Though big enough to house scores of monks, it had the air of a small Greek chapel, with its round turrets and tiny windows.

"Jesus," she said.

When they reached the entrance they were greeted by a group of other tourists, Americans and Australians. A sign was posted by the door: "Women must please cover their heads and wear skirts. Entrance, 50 drachmas." One of the tourists was cheerfully exploring the garden, wearing only her underpants and a shirt. A young Australian woman pointed to her and said to Kathleen, "It's a good thing Jenny wore a skirt or we'd all be shit-out-of-luck." She grinned. "When you go in you can borrow it too. She won't mind."

A couple, both tanned and blonde, came out of the entrance, he in blue jeans and T-shirt, she in a wrap-around skirt over rolled-up jeans. She wore a baseball cap with Beer Drinkers Make Better Lovers printed on it.

"Well at least I won't need the hat," Kathleen said, touching her scarf.

The Australian went into the garden to talk to the owner of the skirt and, when she nodded, called to Kathleen to put it on and go in with Allan. The others didn't mind waiting until they returned.

Inside it was cool and dark. They were shown up the stairway by a silent man in a brown robe. He led them through winding passageways, past tiny bedrooms with single cots, past slits in the stone wall, the only sources of light. They were shown onto a terrace where they could see nothing but sea and sky, the blue and the light remaining with them when they went back inside.

As their eyes adjusted to the dimness, they followed the monk into a large room with walls of carved oak, hardwood floors, and a plaster ceiling decorated with gold leaf. Among carvings and paintings of various saints, a stylized Christ on the cross loomed from the back, giving off, despite the nails in his hands, a sense of tranquility. The head monk, in black robes and square hat, greeted them silently. His face, with a flat nose and creases around his mouth, was unremarkable except for his eyes. They were warm with laugh lines and shone with a kind of inner joy; they were like coals glowing in a furnace. Allan smiled and shook the monk's hand warmly. Kathleen stood to one side, almost wishing to avoid him. There was something suspicious about such obvious contentment.

He gestured to a tray on which stood three small glasses of a yellow liqueur. Smiling, they raised the glasses in a silent toast and savoured the liqueur in small sips, a mixture of fruit and sunlight. Kathleen felt as if she were swallowing joy, a sort of golden richness, and she could feel it flow into her— what? Being? Soul? Innards? It can't be only the liqueur, she thought. She looked at the Christ's expression, tried to figure out in what form he conveyed his sense of peace, and decided it wasn't so much tranquility she saw there as resignation. His eyes weren't warm, in fact his expression seemed to convey neither suffering nor peace. His crown of thorns looked vaguely uncomfortable, and he seemed to be looking at the ceiling in exasperation as if he were a spectator at a particularly shabby and boring circus. Yet there was a calmness there, in the way he was positioned, relaxed and at ease, certain of his place on his impressionistic cross.

The monk refilled the glasses. This time they raised them high, like soldiers in a Little Theatre play. Kathleen smiled to herself, then warmly at the men. She felt incredibly happy. Everything around her was suffused with brilliance, with lightness. Staring at Allan, she realized that he was certain, that he had a solid certainty of the world and his view of it. Who knows, she thought, maybe it's true. Maybe he's right. She noticed that the monk's hands were calloused and lined with indelible earth. The liqueur glass, held between his coarse fingers, looked as if it were delicate crystal, though the glasses were actually cheap and thick, with flaws and bubbles trapped inside. She smiled at Christ hanging calmly from his cross. She was delighted with them all.

The brown monk appeared, holding another bottle. "You like?" he asked Kathleen.

"Yes, very much."

"You buy?"

"Well . . . how much?"

"Six hundred drachmas."

She hesitated. Ouzo was only around three hundred.

"Five hundred," he said.

She nodded, "Okay," then remembered that okay sounded like the Greek word for no and nodded her head again. "Yes, yes," she said. She smiled again at the head monk as she paid for it and asked, "Can you answer some questions? Are you not supposed to speak?"

The monk shook his head. "I do not speak English."

"But how many monks live here? She pointed to the two monks in turn, counting, "One, two . . . "

"Two," he said.

She was confused, thinking he'd misunderstood. "Um, I mean in the whole building." She swept her arm around as though she were encompassing the world.

"Two," he said again. "We are two monks here."

They finished their drinks in silence. Kathleen felt her joy diminishing, like a balloon with a slow leak, but she couldn't understand why, really, couldn't put her finger on the exact location of the opening. Was it simply because monks like these were dying off? She was slightly irritated with Allan now, who stood beside her shining a little, like a candle. "This little light of mine," she remembered singing as a child.

"I like that you visit," the monk said, blessing them with a wave of his hand. "Thank you. Goodbye."

They walked through the passageways into the sunlight, where Kathleen returned the skirt. "I really appreciate you waiting for me," she said.

"Oh you're very welcome." The girl wound the skirt around her own hips. "I hope the monks didn't have heart attacks seeing me wandering among their zucchinis in my knickers." She smiled and waved to the others, calling them over, and Kathleen felt fine again.

The group was ready to go back, but Allan and Kathleen decided to return in the cool of the evening. They strolled in the garden, loose-limbed and relaxed, toward the olive grove. She took his arm and said, "Thank you for the present." He nodded and touched her hair. She knew he had taken some of the monk's silent joy away with him, and it might be days before it wore off.

Years later, long after the liqueur was finished, long after she'd grown tired of closing her eyes and had left Allan picking bananas on a kibbutz by the Sea of Galilee, she could still conjure up his gift, turn it over in the light and make it sparkle: the image of a monastery like white parchment set against washes of aquamarine and sapphire. She kept the liqueur bottle, too, with a couple of drops of the liquid remaining. Whenever she opened it, she caught an odour of fruit, faintly decayed.

◆

Marx on the Wall

◆

"HARPO," SHE SAID, AND HE BEGAN TO BOUND AROUND THE ROOM, silently bouncing on the couch, galloping over the coffee table. Finally he grabbed her and carried her into the bedroom.

His real name was Drew Pendleton. Drew P., Georgina had thought after their first night in bed. The next day, however, after watching old movies for five solid hours, they'd made love all night. Silently, silently he undressed her, silently he'd been hard inside her, lasting forever. He had become the reincarnation of one of the great stars from the golden age of film.

Now it was two months later, and nothing much had changed, except Georgina's enthusiasm. Tonight they were making love again. "Ohhhh," she moaned.

"Honk. Honkhonkhonkhonk." Drew was honking the bicycle horn he'd hidden under the bed.

"How could I have let this happen?" she asked herself.

◆

The short cold winter days didn't depress Georgina as they did most people. The earlier it became dark the better, as far as she was concerned, because as soon as her small apartment acquired the proper density of gloom, she could begin to watch films.

She had started to become a movie fanatic when she was fourteen, sitting in the local cinema or watching TV, feeding herself junk food automatically, her arm like an assembly line mechanism, her eyes glazing over, all five-foot-ten, two hundred pounds of her longing to be Tammy, Gidget, Patty. She wanted to be cute and tiny, to be able to lose herself in a crowd. Every day in school she was reminded of her size, her lack of grace. All she wanted was escape, and she could do that watching movies or television. Although movies were the best escape, not only did they cost money, but she had to go out in public. She usually went in after the lights were out and the cartoon was playing, and then snuck out again just before the credits started rolling. This habit continued even after she left home to live in the city, even after she lost over sixty pounds.

After she'd been on her own for awhile, the weight just seemed to disappear. She grew her thick dark hair long for the first time in her life. She realized she'd become reasonably attractive but never lost the desire to be cute and anonymous, to blend in. Her clothes were never quite in style; she bought everything on sale, usually at Sears. She wanted nothing more than to look as if she'd stepped off the pages of last year's catalogue.

She had worked for a few years typing and filing for a government insurance agency before deciding to look for another job. Getting work in a library film department was, she thought, the luckiest break of her entire life, and she'd been there now for just over a year. She was absent-minded, though pleasant enough with her co-workers and the patrons who came in to borrow films and projectors. For the few months, however, since she'd been able to take one of the library's old projectors home with her, work had become nothing more to Georgina than a period of waiting, a necessary part of daily existence that must be endured before her real life began.

Her favourite films had always been the golden oldies. The projector would be plugged in immediately after her evening meal and she'd be drawn into whatever world was flashed onto her cream-coloured wall. Her favourite was *Casablanca*: Just thinking the name could lift her into *Here's looking at you kid, the war, the war, cigarettes without guilt, oh, is that cannon fire or is it my heart pounding*? She was ready to play it again, for the seventh time, when she brought home *Duck Soup* by mistake.

She had been looking forward to Bogart and Bergman all day, but now she realized that one of the staff had either made an error while helping to pack up the films, or played a joke on her. She stared blankly at the words "Marx Brothers" as the four characters grinned at her from the square of light on the wall.

Shit, she thought, who was that idiot with the—painted! That moustache was painted on his face for God's sake. They all knew she hated comedies. Somebody had done this on purpose. What an awful dance number. Was this sick or what. Puns! God, she couldn't believe it. What was that? That wig was too much. Really. Wait, she thought, that face.

A loony scarecrow, glowing with hilarity, bounded, galloped into the scene radiating fiendish joy one minute, outrageous ferocity the next. What was he doing with those scissors, with that horn? She began to smile. Snip. There was no *reason* to any of this. Honk! It was unreal; his leg, ha, she snorted, what was he doing with his leg? Now he was in the lemonade, oh no, she laughed helplessly, THAT FACE! His cheeks puffed out like a demented gopher, eyes crossed, lips fishily grotesque (this, she discovered when she read his autobiography, was Harpo's famous "gookie"). By this time she was gasping, tears running down her face. She was amazed that such a being could exist.

Georgina watched the rest of the movie waiting for Harpo, cursing the director for not giving him more time. She rewound the reels and played the entire film over again, stopping the projector after every Harpo scene, backing up the reels and watching each one over and over.

The next evening, she brought home A Night at the Opera. Yes, there he was again, his wig of silly curls surrounding his hopeless-case face, tattered trenchcoat containing everything from hot coffee to live animals. Absurd, totally unreasonable, hilarious as last time but then—What was this; he was playing his harp. She waited for his face to light up with loony merriment, waited for him to clip the harp strings with a wire cutter, for him to start playing with his toes. But no, he continued to play music, and his face became radiantly peaceful, serene and joyful. In Harpo's face these words became solid, regained their beauty, their originality. His hands caressing the harp were extensions somehow not only of Harpo Marx but of peace and joy. Georgina fell in love.

Harpo and his surreal craziness, his gentle mute lunacy. She took home a Marx Brothers film every night and played Harpo's scenes over and over. She became familiar with every expression on his face, every one of his moves. She began to tell library patrons that no Marx brothers films were available. The characters she used to love from all the golden oldies became nothing. Gloria Swanson in *Sunset Boulevard*; Marlene Dietrich and her ruined professor in *The Blue Angel*; Lon Chaney's Hunchback; Clarke Gable, Bette Davis; even Bergman and Bogart: all were forgotten. Eventually, she pretended to send out all the Marx Brothers films on interlibrary loan to a hamlet somewhere north of Prince Albert. (They were safely stacked under her couch, each one curled up like a steamrollered cartoon cat.)

She stocked up on junk food just as she had done when she was a teenager, forgetting her diet. She would have taken the phone off the hook every evening if she'd expected any calls. Now her day didn't really begin at all until after work, when she was once more at home in her apartment, waiting for dusk. Then she would put a film on the projector and start in on the potato chips, laughing hysterically, swooning at Harpo in boxer shorts and undershirt, swooning again during his harp scenes, wanting, no, panting to be held in those arms, those arms; playing scenes over and over again, lying on the couch yes yes again and again to harp music. Then once more being carried away into insanity, onto a roller coaster of mad hilarity, rolling on the floor, breathless from spasms of helpless laughter.

It was at the end of the second month of her discovery of the Marx Brothers that she noticed a poster on the library bulletin board. It said, "Marx Brothers in *A Night at the Duck Races*, the movie nobody's seen." Only one showing, that night, university theatre.

She did not relish going to movies alone any more, especially since she'd become used to watching them in the comfort and privacy of her own living-room. She had never grown used to crowds or social events, but this of course was different. This was a special occasion.

Her hands were damp with nervousness by the time she got to the theatre. She was determined to sit in the front row since, compared to those in the regular theatres, the university film screen was small. She walked in, hesitated, then went to the bathroom instead. The theatre was already full of people. Finally, awkward and self-conscious, she walked the long gauntlet to the front of the room. She collapsed into the first front row seat available, not noticing anything but the fact that she was finally out of the public eye.

The movie began. "No wonder it's the movie nobody's seen," said a guy behind her. It was one of the Marx Brother's later efforts; the madcap enthusiasm just wasn't there.

"Chico needed money for his gambling debts so they made this turkey," someone commented. People started to walk out. But where was Harpo? Not until the middle of the movie did he finally appear, but when he did, Georgina forgot everything and roared with laughter. The man beside her, who had been sitting stiff and silent throughout the first half, now howled and slapped the back of her chair. She didn't mind, Harpo had just given his leg to Chico, trampled some flowers, pulled a piglet out of his trenchcoat, and escaped from a policeman in the back of an ice wagon, giving the audience a gookie as he sat down on a block of ice.

Georgina and her neighbour were in hysterics, choking, falling out of their chairs, tears streaming down their faces; they were helpless as baby hyenas. They leaned on each other, slapped each other's backs, gave each other Kleenex until the movie was over. The lights went on and, as they helped each other out of the empty building, the man said, "We should at least go somewhere for coffee. My name's Drew."

"Mine's Georgina," she said, feeling suddenly awkward.

"Film department?" Drew stirred and stirred his coffee. "You have all the Marx Brothers movies?"

"All the best ones, yes. In fact," she said, feeling a confidential glow, "I have them in my apartment."

"Would you like to go out with me tomorrow night?" he asked. "Or maybe I could come over?"

He had shown up at her door wearing a curly strawberry-blonde wig and a tattered trenchcoat. He looked remarkably like Harpo, and she was delighted, appreciating the effort he'd made to produce such authentic detail. Then she noticed the suitcase. "You don't want to move in do you?" she asked, wary but for some reason passive.

He nodded mutely, pointed to his mouth and rubbed his stomach.

She should have known better. She'd never lived with a man before, but had enough experience to know she would likely find it difficult. Not to mention she didn't know Drew from Adam. Then she thought it could prove to be interesting, especially since they seemed to have so much in common. "Okay," she sighed. "I'll at least fix something to eat. Then we'll see."

At first, she didn't mind his horsing around, and he was, even though he had to work himself up to it, a good lover. He was usually still asleep when she left for work in the mornings, and when she came home, he was always Harpo: wig, coat, underwear and all. At least he was quiet. But he became more and more abrasive. He couldn't play the harp, and Harpo's musical interludes were the only scenes which he didn't appreciate or try to imitate. He began to irritate Georgina whenever Harpo played music, and would interrupt her during these scenes, on purpose.

The evening she was watching *A Night in Casablanca* was the last straw. She waited, waited, she knew exactly when Harpo was to come onto the screen, and then there he was and her heart melted; yes, she thought, that was exactly what happened, those were the exact words to use, her heart was melting. His face was peacefully glowing, his fingers caressing, oh tenderly caressing the harp strings (my heart strings, she thought, in spite of herself) playing impossibly, beautifully— Drew bounded into the room, flung popcorn to the four corners of her apartment and made hand shadow animals on the wall where the film was shining. Later, of course, there was the bicycle horn under the bed.

She remembered the time when she had wished and wished for a Barbie Doll with a wardrobe, and had received instead a Barbie-type doll of cheap plastic with a collection of clothes made by her mother. She had tried, sensibly, to play with the doll but finally preferred to moon once again over the pictures of real Barbies in the catalogue.

♦

"People are becoming suspicious," Georgina said, giving Drew an earnest look across the table. "My boss can't understand why anybody from Love, Saskatchewan would want to hoard our entire collection of Marx Brothers movies. I'm going to take them back tonight."

"What!?" He was shocked into eloquence.

"You can help me put them in the car. I want to get them back before they lock up the building."

"You can't be serious," he whined.

"Oh? Would you rather I lost my job *and* the films?"

They returned the films to the library. That night they turned on the TV. Drew paced the floor, wandering through the small rooms, trying, with his sullen face, to grate on Georgina's nerves. He refused to take off his Harpo costume. Georgina remained calm, and allowed herself a slight smile whenever he paced into another room. Finally, after three days, she came home once again to an empty apartment. Nothing was left of Drew but a few strands of vinyl hair on her pillow.

She went to her closet, took out a box she'd hidden the week before and opened it. She connected the new machine to her television and put one of the video cassettes into the slot as reverently as a priest slipping the Host into the mouth of an important parishioner. To her relief, it worked just as well as the new VCRs in the library. She could fast-forward, she could rewind, she could stop and hold. The remote control was a magic wand, a sceptre that bestowed upon her a silent power.

Harpo, glowing with hilarity, with fiendish glee, bounded, galloped onto the screen, radiating joy. On the wall where she used to show movies, Georgina had hung two posters. One was of Harpo making a gookie, the other, Harpo again, caressing his instrument.

Bliss Symbols

I RIDE THE DISABILITIES COUNCIL BUS TWICE A WEEK, NOT BECAUSE I need it myself, although I'm certainly not as spry as I once was, but because I'm a volunteer. After my children had been gone for a few years, I decided I'd do something useful, rather than take more art history classes at the community college.

I accompany senior citizens on their way to therapy sessions at the rehab centre. Once I'm there, I spend an hour or so in speech therapy with a little boy named Jason. Other volunteers don't usually enjoy working with Jason, because there never seems to be any real response from him. He's a gangly kid, all arms and legs, with a scrawny little humped back. He is autistic, whatever that is, and blind, and his spine is somehow crooked, damaged so that he has no strength in his limbs. His hands are able to grasp objects lightly but with no real enthusiasm, much in the way he himself seems to grasp reality. If he is left alone, he will spend his time rocking back and forth, reciting advertising jingles. He knows when there are people near him, and if you give him a hug, he sometimes responds with a little inward grin. He will often giggle to himself, a light chortle that seems to come from some active naughty little boy buried under the layers of disabilities.

We play games together designed to encourage him to say words in context. In one activity, he's supposed to describe objects I put in his hands: hard, soft, rough, smooth, warm, cold. Instead, he sometimes seduces me into his own sing-song rhythm. I hand him a piece of rock and say, "Rough! Heavy!" and he sings, "Ruff, hayevy, ruff, hayevy." I hand him a satin pillow and say, "Smooth, soft," and he'll chant, "Smoooth, sawft." Once in awhile, he'll perk up like a little rabbit sniffing the air and say, "Did you fart?" and present me with one of his giggles. I overreact and laugh, "What?! No way, it must have been *you*." He'll say, "No, it was you," and retreat once again into his cocoon. I have no illusions that this is any kind of real exchange. It's a sequence of words he's learned, and for some reason the reactions he gets or the words themselves give him enough pleasure to repeat them.

I remember once, when my son Victor was three years old, he was going out with his dad for a car ride to visit somebody. He yelled, "Goodbye, Mom!" and I got to the door just in time to see him run jauntily down the walk in his cowboy hat, enough of a toddler yet to have a hint of hope in his voice as he said, with a loud teasing question mark, "It's my turn to drive, *right, Dad?*" For some reason this precipitated one of those moments when I had to sit down, I felt overwhelmed by waves of love that left me helpless, like a turtle washed onto its back. I was only beginning, in those years, to learn to live with the knowledge that if anything happened to my children only my shell might be left.

I have a real affection for little Jason, but I say that knowing full well he could move away tomorrow and I wouldn't be particularly unhappy, and as for him, he doesn't likely recognize me from day to day. He knows my name, though; it's become one of the words that inhabit his inner world. When he hears my voice he greets me, overstressing the first syllable, as if he were beginning to say "Alice, how wonderful to *see* you again," only he says just my name, and only once. "Alice," he says, when I come in and I'll say, "Jason. How are *you* today?" but by this time he's back inside himself.

The real reason they have a problem finding volunteers to work with Jason, I think, is because of the sight of his eyes. That is, one eye is rolled back white in its socket, and the other is missing altogether. He has left eyelids and tear ducts but no left eye. I don't know why it doesn't bother me; I've never been particularly tough-minded about physical abnormalities. I just find everything about him comfortable. I like to think we have an understanding, that we are friends.

I often wonder what is in store for him, what will happen to him when he grows up. I expect likely more of the same. He may reach the age of thirty-five and another volunteer will be going through the same exercises, with him chanting, "Smoooth, haarrd, hayevy," as he loosely clutches a stone egg in his fingers.

Most of the people who ride the disabilities bus are senior citizens. The other, younger ones are mainly accident victims or people who were struck with debilitating illnesses when they were already adults, although there are a few who have been, like Jason, born handicapped. One of these is a man who has cerebral palsy. He can't speak, but communicates by pointing, sometimes with difficulty, at symbols on a desk top attached to the front of his wheelchair. They are called Bliss Symbols, after the man who developed them, who changed his name from Blitz during World War II. I saw a film about him once, at the centre.

Getting on and off the bus must be nerve-racking if you're in a wheelchair. The other passengers who are already strapped into their seats, their canes or walkers beside them, or whose wheelchairs are already locked into position, become tense and silent. The newcomer ascends like an acolyte entering some kind of purgatory; all of us on the bus together remind me somehow of a painting by Brueghel, or maybe Goya. Everybody observes the driver's back and leg muscles as he manoeuvres the chair off the lift and into a place on the bus.

No two bus rides are ever the same, although all the bus drivers seem to have passed some kind of test requiring them to be consistently jolly. Luckily, as far as volunteers are concerned, nobody seems to care if we're not rays of sunshine as long as we show up.

I walk to the senior citizens' home near our house every Tuesday and Thursday afternoon, and wait in the lounge near the entrance for anyone who has to go to the rehab centre. For the last few months, it's usually been Ned, who's had a stroke. Even though he's seventy-five, in poor health and may drop dead tomorrow, he's taking speech therapy. I don't think his heart is in it. I think he just passively accepts any energy people are willing to expend on him, and maybe likes to get out now and then, even if it's only from one institution to another. It takes awhile for Ned and me to get on the bus because he walks in tiny little steps like the dirty old man on the old "Laugh In" series. The resemblance ends there, however. He has a brushcut, is always dressed neatly in tie and sports jacket, and he exudes goodwill and Old Spice. I especially like him because we don't have to make conversation. We give each other the odd pleasant look, and are otherwise free to sit on the bus and gaze off into space, or listen to other people talk.

The bus rarely goes directly to the centre; it criss-crosses the entire south side of the city sometimes, picking up various people who have made arrangements to use the service. One Thursday soon after I'd started volunteering, it drove to a big house that has been renovated for use as a group home for the handicapped, or rather, the disabled. The word "handicapped" has long been replaced, but I'm still getting used to saying "disabled." "Handicapped" replaced "crippled," which is considered hopelessly derogatory, and I never use it any more. "Disabled," however is already being replaced by "physically (or mentally) challenged," which is a term I know I'll never be able to manage spontaneously, except perhaps in reference to myself. Sometimes I find it a physical and mental challenge getting out of bed in the morning.

Two young men in wheelchairs were waiting outside the group home, and it wasn't until the bus driver had backed the first one onto the lift and into the bus that I realized both men were quadraplegic. The bus driver was in a bit of a hurry, I think, and maybe didn't manoeuvre the second man well enough onto the centre of the lift. Whatever the reason, once he was up and the driver tried to back him in, the wheelchair slipped forward and the driver almost lost his grip. Part of the chair rolled off the edge, and the young man's head fell forward, the rest of him strapped in, his hands hanging useless as dead eagle claws. An attendant from the home ran up just in time to grab the front of the chair and push it back on the lift. Everyone glanced furtively out the windows at the cement sidewalk below. The young man lifted his head up again, with some difficulty. All this happened in a matter of a few seconds, and his friend commented, "Holy shit, Jack, it's a good thing you're an old bronc rider, eh?"

He replied with a weak grin, trying to recover with as little fuss and concern as possible. The bus driver was visibly shaken, and remained uncharacteristically silent throughout the ride to the centre.

The two men eventually started to joke back and forth about a night they'd spent in the bar recently. They were tall men, big-boned, with shoulders that only recently had lost breadth. Their faces were handsome and animated, their voices radiated sex and energy. I didn't pity them at all right then, they were so full of hilarity and bitter strength. Only in retrospect do I wonder how often they wish their accidents had killed them. They remind me of my son.

We have two children, Victor and Valerie. We had no intention of being cute with the two Vs, we just liked both names. They are two years apart; Victor is younger.

Valerie has always done all right. She goes through rough spots, but has the capacity to create a certain serenity that ensures her survival. I don't worry about her; more to the point, I don't want to worry about her. We have an unspoken agreement that when we visit we don't discuss her problems. We talk about books or money, gossip or ideas. We have never had anything but a mother-daughter relationship. It's never occurred to us to want to be friends. I realize sometimes that she may need to tell me personal things that are depressing her, but I don't want to know about them unless they have to do with her physical health. In return, I agree not to go on and on about Victor.

Victor has already wrecked his marriage, and has never been able to hold down a job for any amount of time. He's been an alcoholic now for years. He started coming home from parties at sixteen, stumbling through the dark, reeking of hard liquor, sick as a dog sometimes. We worried, we yelled, we talked to him. "All the kids drink," he said. "I only do it once in awhile." We grounded him and he snuck out without us knowing. I realize now that we were deliberately blind; we had simply run out of options and didn't know what else to do, finally, but ignore it. "It's a stage," I said. "He's already an alcoholic at eighteen," his father said, and we couldn't do anything but hope he'd smarten up. He finally flunked grade twelve and started coming home drunk and obnoxious, and we kicked him out. He came back to live, two years later; he was down and out, said he'd quit drinking and wanted to go to technical school. He stayed six months, the same thing happened, we kicked him out.

It has all happened over and over again. He married and had two kids. His wife left him, said there'd been domestic violence, that he'd hit her. I didn't believe that. When neither of them had jobs for awhile, we took in the whole family for four months and there was never anything of the sort. He didn't drink at our house though. He'd take his unemployment cheque and rent a hotel room by himself and have a drunk every few weeks, telling us he was going up to Prince Albert to look for work. Finally they moved into low-rental housing in another city where his wife got a job. A few months later, she left him and moved to B.C. with the kids, where she's now living with another man. We never see our grandchildren. I would like to meet her new man just once. I like to think I could tell whether or not he is a decent person.

The last time we saw Victor was two years ago. Donald was saying enough was enough, but I couldn't help taking him in again. "He's our son," I said. Don hadn't retired yet, and was away giving a paper at a convention. Victor chose one of those days to come home drunk in the afternoon and searched the house until he found the bottle of Scotch I'd hidden as soon as he'd shown up. I got home late, as I'd gone over to a friend's place for supper after my volunteer work. Victor was pacing the floor and began shouting about how inconsiderate I'd been for not phoning to say I'd be late—but then of course, he said, he was so unimportant, such a nothing compared to Valerie, what could he expect. He went on ranting, becoming really hateful until finally I broke down, yelling and crying. He took the back of my neck in one hand and forced me down onto a chair. That was when I realized if he could touch me, his mother, with force, he was capable and guilty of a lot more. I told him to get out of my house. He went out to the garage and came back with a tire iron, saying he was going to wreck the veranda he'd just helped his dad to repair. I couldn't think of what to do. What would the neighbours think, I wondered in banal panic. I said, "Calm down and come in, we'll have coffee," and he did. I said I had a headache and went to bed. He stayed, pacing the house like a caged animal until late at night, when he left. He came back the next day and apologized, I gave him his stuff and told him never again. I told Donald only part of what happened: that he had threatened violence, not that he actually touched me. We haven't seen him since, but we had to get an unlisted phone number, so Victor can't phone in the night, drunk, spouting hate or self-pity. I've been to the point where I wished he'd make good on one of his promises to kill himself.

The guilt is at times unbearable. Not so much at the fact that he drinks, but that he's capable of violence. To think I have never known how it felt to be a victim of abuse except in the presence of my own son is so shameful, it was such a degrading experience that I wish I could forget he exists. I think of his wife and my grandchildren, what they must have gone through. I can't help wondering what we could have done, what I did wrong, why, even if he has to drink, all this pent-up bitterness is there. Donald was hard on him at times, but no harder than a lot of other parents we know. As for me, I didn't love Valerie more than I did Victor, as he seems to think; if anything, Valerie was Donald's child and Victor was mine.

Donald hardly ever mentions Victor any more. He just says there's always hope Victor will join Alcoholics Anonymous and straighten out, but I know that's not going to happen. People in AA are convinced to rely on a higher power, and we taught our children that there is no higher power than your inner self. It never occurred to me that one's core may be naturally weak; that my son would never be able, for whatever reason, to rely on himself. He learned from us to consider religion as existing for the spiritually inadequate, and he will never be able to have faith in anything. This is mainly my fault. I wish now I had presented him with options, had truly given him a choice, been more noncommittal about religion instead of making fun of it. Making fun is such an innocent-sounding term for something which has such power to destroy.

I try to live my life and not dwell on all this. Donald and I do some travelling in the winters, and we see Valerie fairly often. She has recently married a very nice young man, and I am hoping for more grandchildren, although she has passed, as she says, the big three-oh. Otherwise, I have my volunteer work.

Last week, the volunteer co-ordinator gave us people who work with children a little pep talk. Pep talk is not the correct term, really, as it was something closer to the opposite. If we're talking to a child's parents, she said, never encourage any illusions, any unrealistic hope. For example, she said, if a child is both physically and mentally disabled, most parents accept the physical disability, but are always seeing signs of intelligence that simply aren't there. They're always hoping that somewhere inside their child is another Christy Brown of *My Left Foot*, who will, if not type a best-selling autobiography, at least learn to communicate.

She didn't look directly at me as she was speaking, but I felt as if the talk came about because of my meeting Jason's parents. After one of my sessions with Jason, as I was getting ready to say goodbye, his mother and father came in. It's strange how all this time I'd assumed Jason was kind of funny-looking because of his disabilities. But in walked his dad, a man of about thirty-five with the same look on his face and the same gangly body, although upright and useful. He even had a slight curve in his back, as if he'd rounded his shoulders in sympathy with his son.

I spoke at some length about how much I enjoyed working with Jason, and we compared notes. I mentioned a feeling I had about him. "You know it's funny," I said, watching Jason's dad help him with his jacket, "but I'm sure, somehow, that Jason has a real sense of humour."

The mother is a sturdy, matter-of-fact person, who didn't strike me as being given to self-delusion. "We know," she said. "We've always known that. You can't tell anything to these professionals, though."

But after all, I thought during the co-ordinator's little talk, is saying that a kid has a sense of humour the same as saying he's intelligent? You don't have to be particularly brilliant to appreciate John Cleese banging his head on the driveway in front of Fawlty Towers, or the Marx Brothers in a chase scene.

On the other hand, in Jason's case a sense of humour would indicate some kind of contact with the world outside himself. Or would it? Can someone be born with an aura of humour? Maybe his inner world is composed of a garden of private jokes in which he's so content to wander around, he doesn't want to come out. Aside from all that, is it so terrible to encourage parents to hope? It's when hope is abandoned, gone altogether, that you realize the gaping emptiness left in its place.

One of the things Donald and I used to do with the kids when they were teenagers was rent projectors and movies from the library. Often, we'd get a half-hour rerun of the "Fawlty Towers" series to start off the evening. We haven't seen any of them since that time, even though we could get them out on video now. I still, however, remember most of the details of our favourite, called "Basil the Rat." The ending was always the best. The rat's head popping up in the cookie tin and the health inspector's expression did it to us every time. By the time Fawlty's wife looked blankly out the window and commented on the rain, we'd be helpless with laughter, holding onto each other's shoulders or slipping down in our seats, no matter how often we'd seen it. Victor got such a charge out of the anagrams made out of the Fawlty Towers sign. Farty Towels was one I remember. Another was Flowery Twat which, Donald and I said at the time, was going a bit far.

It was Valerie, though, who loved jokes and puns. I remember her at ten or so telling the same joke over and over to anyone who'd listen, usually Victor, and they'd both, whether Victor understood the humour or not, go off into conniptions. Their favourite was the one about two carrots crossing the road. One is hit by a truck. The other carrot rushes his friend to the hospital, and after a few hours, the doctor comes into the waiting room. "Will he be all right?" the carrot asks, and the doctor says, "Well, he'll live, but he's going to be a vegetable for the rest of his life."

I have a recurring dream that I realize is horrifying. I'm not even telling the truth here; it's not a dream but a fantasy, a daydream. I picture Victor after driving drunk and having a car accident, in a wheelchair, permanently crippled. I take care of him at home for awhile and then he graduates to a group home. I take him out every day; we go for coffee, we rent "Fawlty Towers" videos. He can't drink alcohol any more. Maybe he can't even talk, and he has a board attached to his wheelchair. Together we ride on the disabilities council bus and learn Bliss Symbols by heart.

♦

June's Night

♦

HE STOOD UP FROM THE TABLE, ORDERED ANOTHER BEER AND crossed the smoky room to the shuffleboard, his walk a mixture of long-legged American cowboy swagger and straight-backed Canadian farmer strut. His wide shoulders became tense as he bent over the game; his narrow hips touched the edge of the board. He moved like a tomcat: graceful. He had a compact bum that fit into his jeans like a peach in its skin. June imagined her hands cupping those Levi pockets; she glanced across the table at Sandra and licked her lips. "Yum," she said.

Sandra and June had taught in the same school for two years before establishing more than a working relationship. They became friends one Saturday in late spring, after they had gone to the beach and spent the afternoon playing "Name That Bird," a game that arose from the science lessons they'd been preparing. It involved surveying the beach scenery and categorizing the various men: a blond-tufted Frisbee catcher, a speckled geek, a gross-bellied beersucker, a common spouse, a furtive nutscratcher. They had come up with a list of fifty-five names, some in better taste than others.

They often went out for a few drinks somewhere, and took turns choosing the bar. Sandra always chose what June referred to as Yuppie Haven, and June chose a place Sandra called Greaseball Junction. Tonight was June's night.

Sandra discreetly examined the cowboy, then shook her head at June in amusement bordering on exasperation. "I've seen you do this a hundred times," she said. "They're always losers. Why don't you face the fact that you're middle class? That you like listening to jazz and going to the art gallery once in awhile? You never go out with anybody you've got anything in common with."

"But it's not my fault," June replied, her eyes still on the cowboy's shoulders.

And it was true. A nice bum in blue jeans or wide shoulders in a checkered shirt or calloused hands and roughly veined, muscular forearms: they did it to her every time. Truck drivers, cowboys, construction workers, she didn't care what kind of work they did as long as they were lean and muscular. And not lean and muscular from working out at the Y after office hours, or jogging before a hot shower and jacuzzi at some club or other. They had to use those muscles to make their living.

It was all, she had decided after years of psychoanalyzing herself in the bar with her friends, her father's fault. He had been a wispy sort of man who liked her well enough, but could never work up any real enthusiasm for anything. He was a pharmacist, and she vaguely remembered him fading in and out of the living-room, quietly asking for the salt at suppertime and absently walking out of the house every morning, headed for the drugstore. He'd grown paler and paler; she remembered his fine moustache over pale pink lips, the thin lock of sandy hair hanging over his white forehead. Finally he faded away altogether and left June and her mother alone.

Her mother had been bewildered for awhile. She didn't know exactly why he'd gone, but discussed things with eleven-year-old June as she would have with a slightly naive adult, and eventually they both decided they'd get along fine. They used the term "not all there" sometimes when they referred to him, but they didn't mean that he was crazy.

June wanted to think of a man as someone she could lean on; someone who was the proverbial tower of strength even though she knew men weren't like that. In grade seven she began to fantasize about men she saw on television or in the movies. Johnny Cash and his slicked-back hair and gravelly voice; Kris Kristofferson with his warm easy-going grin; Clint Eastwood, hard and cool and diamond-eyed; Little Joe Cartright, curls blowing in the wind as he galloped over sagebrush with his six-shooter and brilliant smile. The word *man* began to conjure up a picture of someone who fought hard, worked hard and loved hard; someone whose toughness was tempered by an endearing sweetness. Even though she knew he didn't exist, he came to her bed night after adolescent night. When she grew up, she began to try to find him.

The urban cowboy glanced up from his game and saw her looking; he grinned, his smile charming, a bit lopsided, teeth white against his tanned face. He winked at her; there was a dent in his cheek that would turn into a dimple once she fattened him up a bit, she thought. She blushed and turned away, then smiled to herself. The jukebox crooned and whined: *Sometimes it's hard to be a woman / Givin' all your love to just one man.*

He was crossing the room, his long legs and black boots coming closer and closer until finally he stood over her, looking down at her with his cat's eyes, his crotch at eye level, the shadow of his shoulders falling across her.

"Can I buy you ladies a drink?" he said.

She knew how the conversation would go; she hadn't had hundreds, as Sandra complained, but she'd had quite a few. She'd tell him that she taught grade three, and he'd say, "A schoolteacher, eh?" with a quick grin and have some story to tell about something that had happened to him in elementary school, ending up with a comment to the effect that he sure wished there'd been teachers like her when he was in school. Then he'd tell stories about his work and about crazy things he'd done when he was a teenager. Toward the end of the evening, if he were especially dull or very drunk, out would come the old saw about how maybe she could teach him something.

She smiled up at him and invited him to sit down. She noticed that Sandra was smiling too and was obviously prepared to make the best of things. Tammy Wynette's voice rose an octave or so.

"My name's Ainsley Cameron," he said.

"I'm June and this is Sandra." She could almost feel those hands, the calloused palms rubbing her back, touching her breasts; she wanted to play with the dark fuzzy hair on his chest and arms.

She daydreamed in silence while Sandra, who was usually so self-possessed, awkwardly made conversation. "We're both teachers," she was saying. "June teaches grade three and I teach grade seven."

"Grade seven," he laughed. "You must be a tough lady. I remember the grade seven class I was in drove three teachers loony in one year."

Sandra brightened, and June stared at the ceiling preparing herself for a litany of junior high horror stories. She shifted in her chair, watching him, noticing the muscles of his neck and shoulders move every time he lifted his beer glass. She caught his eye again; this time he looked away first. She had never, she thought, been this horny in her entire life. How was she going to last until he finally drove her home? She crossed her legs and looked around the room. The jukebox was still playing nasal country and western. *She's a good-hearted woman / In love with a good-timin' man.*

June smiled to herself again and looked happily at . . . What was his name? Ainsley. She noticed a group of businessmen sitting at one of the tables and looked them over. There must be some kind of convention going on in this hotel, she thought. There was always something about men in business suits that seemed ridiculous to her. Even on weekends they couldn't relax: they put on T-shirts with collars and jeans that had been ironed. Bank managers, government workers, accountants, lawyers, teachers; they all possessed a pedestrian sameness.

She remembered her first real affair with a "working class hero," as Sandra liked to refer to them. She always remembered it as an affair, even though it lasted only one weekend.

In high school there had been ordinary fumblings in cars with various boys; she had lost what little virginity she had left after her grade twelve graduation party. But it wasn't until the summer of her second year at university that she met Lorne.

She had been lying on the beach at Katepwa in the hot July sun eating sunflower seeds and feeling at one with the universe. The salt taste of the seeds and the sun soaking into her skin like the Coppertone she had rubbed on herself made her feel golden; she felt as if warmth and light were radiating from her body. And then she had opened her eyes, squinting against the sun, and there he was, emerging from the greenish water like— June looked at Ainsley, comparing the two. Who would he have been like? Neither Hercules nor Adonis ever rose out of any water as far as she knew. Neptune? No, he was too old. The frog prince? She was getting drunk.

Lorne had driven her home that day in his big Mercury with the little air freshener fir tree dangling from the rearview mirror. She couldn't remember a word either of them had said the entire weekend. Neither of them could quit smiling; they had looked at each other through a haze, a soft fog. She'd gone to her summer class on Monday feeling voluptuously soft and beautiful. The professor read John Donne: *I wonder, by my troth, what thou and I / Did till we loved?* She'd felt like Aphrodite, like Venus with arms; she opened them and floated home only to find an empty apartment and a poorly written note. At least he didn't fade away slowly, she thought.

She began to listen again to Ainsley and Sandra and was only vaguely aware of the music from the jukebox, Ricky Scaggs singing something about home towns. Considering that Sandra had to be dragged in here, she thought, she certainly seems to be enjoying herself. Sandra and Ainsley were laughing over some of the jokes her grade sevens had told her.

"What do you call someone with no arms and no legs, lying in front of a door? Mat. Lying in a bunch of leaves? Russell. Water skiing? Skip. Hanging on the wall? Art." They were snorting with laughter and June watched them both, smiling, taking another drink of beer. This is taking too long, she thought. Then she realized from the way he was looking at Sandra that she'd lost him.

She looked quickly down at her beer, and up again at Sandra's now obvious fascination with Ainsley's shoulders. She wanted to give her a vicious kick under the table. June noticed for the first time that Sandra's vivacious smile showed eyeteeth that were rather unusually pointed, giving her a predatory look. She admitted to herself that she could have made more of an effort to keep up her end of the conversation, but still, this was too much. This was supposed to be her night.

She took another drink and decided it didn't matter. That's life, she thought, they all disappear into the sunset or cannonball down the road in a cloud of dust. "Hey Sandra," she said. "Been to any good art galleries lately?"

Sandra paid no attention. She was laughing at Ainsley's punch-line:

" 'You're Thor!' the maiden said. 'What about me? I'm tho thor I can hardly pith.' "

Border Lines

IF I WERE EVER PUT IN JAIL, THERE WOULD BE ONE CONSOLATION that would go a long way towards alleviating my depression: the fact that I could start smoking again. I wouldn't have any choice. I would be put in a cell with Matilda the Hun who would smoke up a storm and keep offering me cigarettes from her pack of Sportsman Kings. I would finally accept one, thinking to myself, Oh well, I'm breathing all her second-hand smoke anyway, why not?

Matilda the Hun would be about a hundred and eighty-five pounds. She'd wear grey sweatshirts with writing on them, with the arms cut out to show her tattoos, and she'd have two side teeth missing. I would gain her respect by describing in detail how I murdered my husband, and she would tell me stories about when she sold drugs in Vancouver. She would be a born-again Christian and we would smoke Sportsman Kings and read Revelations aloud to each other every night before lights out.

I quit smoking because my husband Bob did. It seemed a supportive and healthy thing to do at the time, and since smokers have become society's new lepers, I've never regretted it. I'm especially glad I quit now because of the baby. But once in awhile I long to feel smoke sharp-soft on the back of my throat, forming a cloud in my lungs, soothing my heart.

I don't really have fantasies about murdering my husband. We've had a pretty good marriage so far. Bob is solid and sensible and for the most part thinks himself lucky to have married me. It's only since I've had the baby that he's begun to be critical and mean, as if since I'm at home now, dependent on him, he doesn't need to worry about minor courtesies any more.

One day I was so fed up, I threw one of Tyler's plastic baby bottles across the room. Bob got up and, in a rage, hurled the diaper bag right at me. "Don't you ever," he said. "Don't you ever throw anything at me again."

The next time we had a shouting argument, he threw a bowl of popcorn against the wall. I find that depressing and somewhat frightening. It's as if my tantrum crossed a certain line; because I threw something once, it became an acceptable thing for him to do. I'm afraid this might go on every time we have a fight, until the next line is crossed. I've decided it has to be up to me to cool it. No more tantrums for me, I guess.

Matilda the Hun would have had a job as a waitress in a bar once, where she ended up being a bouncer. She would have all kinds of stories to tell about that. She has three daughters, all with beautiful square-jawed faces. Their picture hangs on the cell wall beside the bunk beds.

My son isn't two years old yet. Every once in awhile, when I'm upstairs for a minute, he sneaks open the fridge, quiet as a kitten, and steals a carton of eggs. When I come back, there is egg all over. If he still has one that's not broken, he'll scurry behind a chair and sit quietly, holding it in both hands, hoping I don't see him. It drives me crazy every time, and I yell at him and banish him to his room, but when it's cleaned up, I give him kissies and cuddles because he's such a cute naughty little boy. I guess that's being inconsistent. I guess I'm sending him conflicting messages. Bob doesn't think I'm a very good mother. He thinks inconsistency is the worst sin in childrearing. He doesn't think I take parenting seriously enough.

Bob and I went together all through high school and then got married. Bob works with computers and I worked in a bank and took night classes, right up until Tyler was born. Now I'm taking a few years to be with my son and to finish my degree. In the afternoons, when he's taking his nap, I do my homework and look out my living-room window at our wide lawn and the neighbour's lovely weeping birch. I spend three nights a week taking classes, so on those nights, Bob gets Tyler ready for bed and I go up to the university.

I told my mother-in-law once that Bob was so good with Tyler, I thought he was a better parent than I. That was a mistake, because she believes it's true anyway and whines to Bob about how absent-minded and inconsistent I am: that I even said so myself. She has a talent for making you feel cozy and confiding, and then stabbing you in the back with your own ammunition. Can a knife be classified as ammunition? Anyway, I should know better by now. Bob never has any qualms about telling me what his mother says about me; he always agrees with her and uses her comments to back up his own.

Maybe, once I was already safe in my cell for stuffing Bob down the elevator shaft at the Sask Power Building, I'd hire Matilda the Hun to do Bob's mom in. Matilda would be getting out soon. She would have a black belt in karate and, more significantly, her own mother-in-law would have died under suspicious circumstances.

The class I'm taking this semester is Greek mythology. I sometimes put myself to sleep at night by going over my favourite myths; I'd like to remember them and be able to tell them to Tyler in my own words, when he's older. The one we've just finished studying, however, is not really suitable material for a bedtime story. It's about Actaeon, a hunter who happened to come across Artemis taking a bath, and stayed to watch. When she noticed him, rather than let him go so he could boast about it to his buddies, she turned him into a stag, and had him torn apart by his own hunting dogs. "Some stag party," a guy in the class commented.

When I'm at my night class, I sometimes think about the mass murder of those fourteen women students in Montreal. The funny thing is, I don't think so much about what I'd have done if I'd been a student in that classroom, I think about the murderer's mother, how she must feel. Why did he hate feminists so much? Is she a feminist? Would she feel guilty and say to herself, "Where did I go wrong?"

I was in Mexico once, a couple of years after Bob and I were married. It's the only holiday I've ever had away from him. We were spending the Christmas vacation at his parents' winter place in Brownsville, Texas: a two-bedroom trailer identical to hundreds of others in the community. I had more backbone then; I was only twenty-one, and the confinement of the trailer and its dreary court, combined with the mild eccentricities of my in-laws was driving me crazy. Bob was away nearly every day playing golf, so I decided to go on a short tour of the nearest Mexican state. My in-laws would have taken me for a trip across the border if I'd have asked, but I was feeling rebellious; I wanted to go alone. Where young women in books travel to exotic places and find themselves in lives of independence and romance—a contradiction in terms if there ever was one—I took a three-day bus tour.

The other tourists were mostly middle-aged Americans. I sat behind a couple in their late fifties named Stu and Bernice, who decided to take me under their wing. Once I was actually on my own I didn't feel very brave, so this was all right with me. Unlike the United States, Mexico is, after all, a foreign country.

That first day, whenever we'd stop at a marketplace, I'd go shopping with Stu and Bernice, and the shopkeepers would ask Stu for permission to show me their blouses and jewellery. They'd start out with what was supposed to be a ridiculously high price and expect me to bargain with them. "I don't like to bargain," I said at one of the first shops and started to leave, but Stu said, "Don't you worry, sweetheart, I'll jew them down for you," and for the rest of the day he handled all my transactions.

That evening we stopped in Tampico and were booked into a pink cement hotel with fans rotating apathetically on the cracked ceilings. Since there were no other single women on the tour, I was given a room of my own. I ate dinner with Stu and Bernice on the restaurant veranda. Cicadas chirped and exotic flowers bloomed on shrubs which shut out the dusty street. I found the spicy food delicious, and was thrilled to be in a foreign country. It did cross my mind, after Bernice started to complain about her digestion, that I might as well be travelling with my in-laws, but still I was grateful for the company. I don't like to eat alone.

I was getting ready for bed later that night, a little tipsy from drinking two margueritas, when somebody tapped furtively at the door. Remembering the appraising look a couple of the Mexican men in the restaurant had given me, I didn't unlock it.

"Who is it?" I said.

"Ssh, it's me," a voice rasped.

"Who's me?" I said, another suspicion beginning to surface.

Dead silence.

"Go away," I said.

The next day I came into breakfast late, when Stu and Bernice were almost ready to go. When Bernice went to pack up their things for the day's bus trip, Stu stayed and had another cup of coffee. He decided on the direct approach. "Are you available?" he asked, looking down and stirring his café con leche.

"No," I said primly, "but if you are I'll let my grandmother know. She might be interested."

He pursed his mouth and looked at me the way he looked at the little Mexican beggars. "There's no need to be insulting," he said. He got up and marched stiffly out of the room. He'd have been even more insulted if he knew both my grandmothers were dead.

We avoided each other for the remainder of the weekend, Bernice seeming to know either by experience or instinct that something had happened. I was afraid of Stu now. I wasn't sure how weird he was, what he'd be capable of doing to revenge his hurt feelings. I felt robbed, and couldn't enjoy anything. At the Aztec ruins I pictured sacrificial blood. I saw nothing but dust, cruelty and poverty in the villages and towns we passed through.

In one of these the tour bus broke down, and we had to hang around the garage half a day waiting for it to be repaired. Towards evening, I wanted a snack, so I brought out a package of cookies that immediately attracted a big-eyed, scrawny little girl. She had emerged from the garage, which was a sky-blue cement square with peeling walls. I ate a couple of cookies and gave the rest to the girl. I expected she'd maybe lose most of them to other kids, but didn't expect a man to come out of one of the huts across the way, grab the whole package and eat the cookies in front of her. Since he talked to her as if he had some authority, I assumed he was her father. He looked right through me and walked away, obviously savouring each cookie, although they were all gone in less time than it took him to reach his hut.

Now, whenever I think of Mexico, I see Stu's face with its flabby jowls asking if I'm available, and I see a man eating cookies in front of a sky-blue garage.

We were late getting back to Brownsville because of the bus breaking down, so it was almost midnight by the time I got to the trailer. Even though I had to cope with Bob and his parents who were beside themselves with worry, I was relieved to be back. I never went anywhere by myself again.

Why the Montreal mass murder reminded me of that trip I have no idea. Maybe the Aztec sacrificial stones, my images of the high priests tearing the hearts out of adolescent girls. They've been interviewing these experts who study serial and mass murderers and comparing the psychology of the two types. When someone on the radio first mentioned serial killers, my mind, in spite of myself, formed a mad picture of a midget in a striped tuque stomping on some Cheerios and Rice Krispies.

Even though none of us eats it, I always cook up a pot of Cream of Wheat first thing in the morning. Bob and I drink coffee as Tyler spreads Cream of Wheat on himself and blops it onto the high chair tray, squishing it between his fingers. Then I clean it up and we start our day. I realized the futility of this exercise months ago, but by that time morning cereal had become a ritual, and Tyler complains until he gets it. I have decided to look on Cream of Wheat as creative material, like finger paint or playdough.

Matilda the Hun likes to paint by number. Each set includes two almost identical paintings, so our cell wall is covered with two winter scenes, two sunsets over the ocean, two horses, and one parrot in a flowered jungle. I smoke a cigarette, watching Matilda paint the other parrot. The paint comes in tiny plastic pots connected together in rows of eight; each colour is carefully mixed with a plasic stir stick which we scrounge from the prison cafeteria. The paint glides off the brush, forming a shining oil slick over each outlined area. Matilda is so precise and has such a steady hand that I can see the blue ink of the outlines between the colours. I smell oil paint and taste Sportsman Kings.

The blue ink of the outlines is a lighter blue than the tattoos she has on her arms. Her tattoos are homemade ones, the kind you can do with a sharp fountain pen. I heard on "Morningside" once that self-mutilation is a big problem in women's prisons, but Matilda's tattoos are nothing like that. She has a high pain threshold, and tattoos are just another way of expressing herself.

Another time, Peter Gzowski interviewed a woman who had lived with an abusive husband. She said her ex-husband used to drink and started out with verbal abuse, but always held himself back from anything physical until one night she went out with friends and came back after a few drinks herself to find him pacing with fury. He called her names until she slapped him. He took great pleasure, she said, in finally feeling able to beat her up. That slap of hers became for him the justification for years of abuse. He had been waiting, and sure enough, she had done something wrong; she started it; she had been the first to cross the border into violence.

I thought about that after Bob threw the bowl of popcorn. It was only a salad bowl of light wood, and didn't do any damage, but it was I who cleaned up the mess. Of course I was the one who'd thrown something in the first place, weeks before. Anyway, I guess when Bob yells at me the next time Tyler gets into the eggs, I'll disappoint him. I'll just quietly clean up and pretend nothing was said. Matilda the Hun would never be much for self-control, but then she's got a black belt in karate.

I know it's no better to make generalizations about men than for them to stereotype us. I know Bob is trying to keep his place on the corporate ladder, that job security isn't what it used to be and he's feeling the pressure of being the sole income earner, the provider for a family. I know there is something ridiculous about being afraid of men like poor old Stu in Mexico, or apprehensive about Bob throwing a bowl of popcorn. Still, sometimes I think men are waiting. They wait for us to provide the last straw, to make the first move, for us to be the first to cross the border. Good women never do, and I'm nothing if not a good woman.

The Inheritance

JOYLENE COULD SENSE THAT SOMETHING WAS GOING TO HAPPEN; some major event was going to alter her life. The Feeling, as she referred to it, came upon her periodically, but she usually tried to ignore it. It was a phenomenon inherited from her grandmother and took various forms, from a prophetic feeling to feeling she could read certain minds to simple feelings of power. She always stifled it, however. She had no curiosity about what was in other people's dirty little minds; she sensed enough about the future already to have no desire to learn the details; and as for feelings of power, they simply made her afraid. This one disappeared as suddenly as it had come, and Joylene walked out of the w.c.

"You'd think that they'd at least have decent toilet paper in an international airport," she said. "It's like wax paper. It's unbelievable, like everything else in this country." Her words were bitter, without a trace of amusement. Her face looked caustic; the delicate prettiness she'd had in her twenties was now sharpened, hatchet-like. The end of her nose always looked cold and pinched, a perpetual reminder of cold Saskatchewan winters.

Her husband, Stanley, glared at her, his irritation so obvious and intense that she sensibly pursed her mouth and took a magazine out of her flight bag.

He'd also had delicate features when he was twenty, or at least so Joylene had thought. But instead of sharpening with age, Stanley's features had blurred: his face became pudgy, his second chin wobbled, his nose was almost completely overpowered by his fat cheeks and horn-rimmed glasses. He was the principal of Crystal Creek Composite High School, and was known to his students as Old Flubber.

They sat, side by side, waiting for their flight number to be called. Joylene listlessly flipped through her magazine, skimming over articles and quizzes. (Can This Marriage Be Saved?) The holiday had been her idea. All Stanley wanted to do was go up to Melfort to visit his family and then spend some time at their cottage at Emma Lake, as usual, even though Joylene always complained about the mosquitoes and was afraid of the water.

Because Joylene's grandmother had been English, she had talked for years about making a trip to the old country, to the Seat of Culture, as she referred to it. After an enormous amount of research concerning her family tree, she discovered that her great great grandmother had been hanged for practising witchcraft and prostitution, and her only living relative in England had chosen a career cleaning toilets and collecting tips from patrons of a public washroom. Joylene had no desire to meet him, but the Seat of Culture still had to be experienced.

Stanley hadn't relaxed for the entire holiday and neither had Joylene, but at first she tried to pretend to be having a good time, since it had been her idea. Stanley drove her crazy moaning through tours of dank castles and museums, sneering at the works of art. The terrible thing was that she was as bored as he with the insipid madonnas holding grotesque babies, or that same fool saint with the arrows stuck in him as if he were a pin cushion, showing up time after time, dreary museum after gallery after museum. They had gone to the opera and the London Symphony, and to the theatre a couple of times; neither of them extracted one iota of entertainment from any of it.

The last straw, the very last straw, was when she discovered Stanley didn't know enough about their new camera to adjust the light meter properly. He had clicked away at every sight they saw without adjusting anything and without saying a word. Her last enjoyment—looking forward to showing slides to neighbours and family—had disappeared like a greasy soap bubble down the drain.

She clutched at her magazine as she remembered the lengths of ruined film and tried to control her breathing. "Think happy thoughts," her grandmother had always said. "Think happy thoughts and you'll never regret it." Joylene remembered some of the songs her grandmother was always singing: "Let the Sun Shine In," "Keep on the Sunny Side," "The Sunny Side of the Street." She let out a deep breath and, looking again at the magazine, read an article about Princess Di. But when she finished it, the Feeling came back, twice as strong as before. She looked straight at Stanley, humming to herself. Stanley, who was looking through her as usual, got up and disappeared into the w.c.

He still had the runs, she thought with satisfaction. The intercom crackled, "Air anada, fight ree fi two is ready for oarding." She looked toward the men's washroom, then at her watch, and began to tap her foot on the floor as if keeping time to music echoing inside her. The Feeling had disappeared.

Finally, after it was announced that their flight would be ready for departure in fifteen minutes, she knocked on the men's w.c., opened the door and called, "Stan. Stanley are you in there? Is anyone in here?" No answer. She walked in and saw nothing but blank white polished urinals, an empty attendant's chair, and a condom dispenser with the words, "Don't buy this chewing gum — it tastes of rubber," scratched on the side. One toilet stall was closed, and she looked under the door to see if she could see any feet. She saw four of them. What would two men be doing together in one cubicle, she wondered vaguely. They knew she was there, they were being deathly silent, and the four shoes were as still as the ceramic boots she had seen once at the Mendel Art Gallery when she was in Saskatoon visiting her brother Alvin.

She stood up; a man came halfway into the washroom, looked at her, said, "Excuse me," and backed out. She was about to walk out when she thought maybe one pair of those shoes looked like Stanley's Hush Puppies. She walked slowly to the cubicle door and bent down for another look. None of the shoes had moved. "Are you in there?" she said.

"Mom?" answered a quavering voice.

The man in the Hush Puppies cleared his throat but didn't say anything. Of course it wasn't Stanley. She looked around uncertainly, noticing that beside the attendant's chair was an ashtray with a stub of a cigarette still glowing, giving off a pale wisp of smoke. The washroom door opened again. This time she caught a glimpse of a face in the mirror; it was like a ghost of a memory, like a spirit flashing across her line of vision. She rushed out of the washroom, but whoever it was had disappeared.

"I was looking for my husband," she said to the four men waiting outside the door.

"American," one man said to the others, and they nodded and trooped into the washroom in a scornful line.

Joylene sat down, feeling as if Novocaine had been injected somewhere into her mind. Had he finally left her? Just disappeared like that? Could he have been mugged? Become really sick? But then she thought, "He got on the plane by himself. I know it. He's pushing it to the limit, he's too afraid to be the one, oh yes he wants *me* to leave." She started up from her chair and walked quickly to the boarding gate. She hesitated before going on, then resolutely boarded the plane. But when she found her seat, there was no one, nobody at all in the seat beside her.

What could have happened to him? What was she going to say to everyone in Crystal Creek? Her mother-in-law and her neighbours and the schoolboard. They had a nice house and she'd never had to work ever, and what was she going to tell Melvin who was going into his second year of computer science this fall? He'd have to get a student loan. What if Stanley disappeared forever and she couldn't collect alimony? Who would support her? The house wasn't even paid for and they used a big chunk of their savings for this stupid trip. A cold fear touched her spine, forcing her to sit rigidly upright. Where could she go? She couldn't live with her parents, they'd sold their house and moved into a small apartment in Melfort. Maybe Melvin would give up university and get a job, and she could live with him.

The plane took off smoothly. She forgot her anxiety for a moment with the feeling of exhilaration she had whenever she began a flight, but started to worry again as soon as the airplane levelled off. She would tell everyone that Stanley had—what? Become ill? Decided to stay awhile longer? But she would be expected to stay with him if he were sick. And simply deciding to stay longer would mean he would have to pay full air fare on the trip back. It wasn't like him to do something like that. No, he had left her, and soon it would all come out.

He had been nice-looking once. Such a gentlemanly type of person, she had thought before their marriage. So different from her father who would hawk and spit as he walked across the yard to milk the cows or fix the combine, and honk his nose like a polite bicycle horn when he was in church. And well-educated. Not like her old boyfriend who always said, "I seen," and, "We don't got none." Stanley, with his fine small hands, intelligent-looking face and good grammar won her over, and they were married after her grade twelve graduation. But he had turned out, she thought, to be a pig in sheep's clothing.

She had always known that sex was as gross with people as it was for cows and pigs, but the fact of it, the actual demands Stanley made of her after they were married disgusted her to distraction. And sex was only the tip of a mountainous iceberg of vulgarity to which he subjected her. He picked his teeth with his fork, he left stains on his underwear, he always left his socks in a soggy pool by the tub, he got whiskers in the toothpaste, he spit into the sink and didn't rinse it out, he broke wind in bed. But it was his nosepicking that drove her half-mad. He never did it in public, thank God. Only when he was relaxed, absent-mindedly reading the paper, would his hand steal up to his chin, fingers playing first with the corner of his lip, then scratching at his nose, one finger finally dominating, the rest curling under while it started to dig into a nostril, seeming to have a lusty life of its own. She couldn't stand it. Every time it happened she watched him for a stunned moment, disgust growing large in her throat like a type of fungus until she finally screeched at him. After a few years he grew fat, and she knew, she just knew, he did that on purpose too because he knew she hated anything gross.

She stared out the window until the plane was enveloped in clouds and she noticed the reflection of a man in the seat behind her. He was reading a paper, his glasses supported by fat cheeks, his finger in his nose. But when she turned around, there was only a skinny little boy with a comic book.

Her nerves had always been bad. "High strung," her mother called her, and she thought of herself that way: a delicate violin, a musical instrument strung to a high pitch ready to shriek if irritated, ready to snap.

If it hadn't been for her grandmother, she believed, she might have gone over the edge. Her grandmother used to talk about the women in their family having something special that showed up every second generation, and without saying anything outright, they both knew she meant The Feeling. Joylene's mother knew nothing about it. Her grandmother looked on it as a curse; as something evil to be fought against with cheery thoughts and prayers to Jesus. Only after she had been admitted to the Nirvana Pioneer Villa in Melfort, did the terrible change come over her. She would look around with sunken pale blue eyes and croak, "Jesus H. Christ, I lost the power. I can't believe I lost it and didn't even use it once." She swore and whined in a senile sing-song until the week before she died, when she said to Joylene, "Don't waste it," and went into a coma.

Joylene had never seriously thought of leaving Stanley. Being divorced nowadays wasn't quite the disgrace in Crystal Creek that it used to be, but aside from all that, what would she do? She had never earned any money in her life and hadn't the faintest clue how to go about finding a job. And now that he was gone, how was she going to collect alimony? What was she going to do if no trace was ever found of him again? What if he were dead? She sat up even straighter in her seat, taking deep breaths to calm herself. Dead. He had good life insurance; her brother Alvin had sold it to him. She looked out at the clouds billowing, swirling softly below her. What was it her grandmother used to say? Every cloud has a silver lining. She would like to rest her head on one of those clouds as she had imagined she could as a child. Rest her entire body on a giant soft cloud, like that Sealy Posturepedic ad they used to have on TV.

It would be so much easier to be a widow. Then she could own the house outright and have enough money to last for the rest of her life, if she got Alvin to invest it for her. She could stay in Crystal Creek or maybe move to Melfort. She would have the sympathy and respect of the community and could perhaps eventually get a nice job somewhere, say part-time at Belle's Style Shop or the post office. She wished the flight would go on and on, and she could sit in this clear sharp sunlight, always looking down on clouds, always alone. She started humming to herself.

She wondered sometimes if The Feeling was real, or if it was something she and her grandmother imagined; maybe they were both crazy. They both had bad nerves, although her grandmother had managed to overcome them and become a pious pillar of the community. During this trip, Joylene had begun to wonder if it was too late to try it out; to see if she really had any power. The problem was, she'd never had any practice, so she didn't know how to go about attempting to use it. She shivered. Maybe she and her Feeling had caused Stanley to disappear in the first place. Maybe her wanting to try it had activated something.

Dinner was served, good Canadian beef in clean plastic. She fell asleep, the first good sleep she'd had since leaving home, and when she woke up, the plane was already landing at Toronto. She felt a shiver of panic. What would she tell people? That Stanley had left her? How would she face anyone?

She had to collect the luggage before she went through customs, and along with a crowd of other passengers, she waited as suitcases were spewn from behind a canvas curtain onto the carousel. She waited as people grabbed their luggage and got in line with their passports. She knew hers would come out among the last, so what else was new? She was beginning to get a headache.

She watched as suitcase after suitcase was claimed by someone, looking, each time new ones appeared, as if she were a tired swimmer seeking a lifesaver. Even if Stanley were dead, she thought, even if she had managed to kill him with her power, it would do her no good unless she could produce his body. She rubbed her forehead. She had a sudden image of this crowd of people leaning forward and gasping. She pictured a pair of legs in dark trousers emerging from behind the canvas, followed by the body of a fat man in a white shirt, his suit coat clenched under one arm, his glasses crooked on his waxen, lifeless face.

"My God, he's dead," someone would say. Nobody would know what to do. Amid a stunned silence, the body would circle around and around with the rest of the luggage.

Indecent Exposure

YOU'LL NEVER GUESS WHAT HAPPENED AT WORK YESTERDAY. Weird things don't usually happen in our office. I mean there's some pretty strange people that come in to apply for UIC and stuff like that, but nobody's ever really *done* anything before. Anyways, there was this guy in yesterday who was hanging around exposing himself. I always wondered what I'd do if anybody ever did that in front of me, you know?

Well, Shirley said that a guy did the same thing to her at a bus stop once. He walked up to her, threw open his coat, you know, just like in the movies, and he said, "What do you think *this* is eh?" in kind of a whiny nervous voice, and Shirley told me she looked at him and said—get this—"It looks like a penis to me, only smaller," and then she walked away, real cool and collected.

Well, I don't know, do you think that she really said that to him? I mean maybe she could've said it, but she wouldn't have acted so calm and cool like she said, right? Really, I think sometimes you can't believe, I mean not that she actually tells lies, like she's my friend and everything, but I really think sometimes you can't believe a thing she says.

Like, one time she told me she was going out with this real hunk, right? So one night I dropped over to her place when I knew he was coming over and jeez what a wimp. I mean, I don't always go out with prime specimens myself but even Harold wasn't as bad as this guy. For one thing he came from Moose Jaw. Yeh, talk about nerd capital of North America, well. So anyways, there I was trying to talk to this gormless wonder for half an hour while Shirley got ready to go out. I could tell she was embarrassed, but what can you do? I'd be embarrassed too if I was so desperate I'd go out with some loser from Moose Jaw and my friends saw him.

Harold? Oh, he was dust two months ago. I only went out with him about five times, just long enough to get to know what a nit he was. He was always forgetting his wallet, you know the type? And let's face it, I only went to bed with him on our fifth date. I thought he was holding off because he was shy, and I thought, *Is this unusual or what*, and then I thought it was kind of cute. So one night I decided tonight's the night, just like in the movies, and so I put on perfume and shaved my armpits and everything, and after the show at the Capitol he brought me home and I invited him in for a drink.

Get this. I lit candles and turned on the stereo, you know, mood music and all that. And when I finally got him into bed he was, you know— He couldn't do anything. He was a nit anyways even not counting that. All he ever talked about was high school and what a good old time he had back in Smuts or wherever his home town was. Yeah he could be a big cheese back in high school, as long as he made sure to go out with girls who wouldn't expect anything.

So there I am, in bed with a loser and wondering what the hell I'm supposed to do with him. I mean he wouldn't say anything even when I asked him questions about it like, "Does this happen often?" He just laid there like some kind of vegetable, looking at the ceiling. I could've used a vegetable right then like a carrot or a cucumber, eh, but there he was, more like a squash. He finally got out of bed, didn't say a word except, "Where's my socks," and left. I haven't seen him since.

Anyways, a few days after that I found out I had an infection and I wondered if frustration can cause it, you know? Then I thought jeez maybe he has herpes or something and that's why he couldn't do anything. That put me in a real panic I tell you, so I finally went to the clinic about it, but it turned out to be nothing.

But jeez. You know when you have an internal and there you are, feet getting cramps in those metal stirrups or whatever you call them and the doctor keeps saying, "Relax dear, just spread your knees and relax." I could gag. And then I always hold my breath when he slips that metal thing in, you know? I'm sure my doctor keeps his in the fridge. Well there I was, looking at the ceiling, counting the little dots on the tiles, just waiting for it to be over, thinking only a couple more seconds, when in comes a couple of *in*terns. And my doctor says to them like he's inviting them to view his stamp collection or something, "Here, have a look at this. It's a classic example of a yeast infection." A classic example, jeez. And there I was, I mean, I just about died.

I felt like a tourist attraction you know? Like the Grand Canyon or something, eh. I was just ready to say something like "Do you mind?" when in comes this nurse who goes, "The plumber's here and he wants to know which office has the plugged sink." Well I was just about crying, I was really pissed off, so I go real loud so I bet they could hear me in the waiting room, "Oh well, ask him to come in why don't you, maybe he'd appreciate a good look too." They all looked up and gawked at me, like they were surprised I had a head.

But what is it with men anyways? I mean, jeez, talk about egos. Old Harold was totally crushed and hates me because he couldn't, and then there's the guys who always have to prove that they can, and think they're real Casanovas. I mean really. There's this guy at work that I do some typing for, he must be fifty-five if he's a day. Well I got to joking around with him you know, thinking of him as a nice old geezer. And then like two days ago, it was secretary's day and he took me out for lunch and then I had the rest of the day off so he drove me home and guess what? Surprise, surprise, he started coming *on* to me, right in front of my apartment building.

I just got pissed off and said if I wanted to get close to fossils I'd go to the Natural History Museum. I mean here's this guy who's been married for thirty years, who got me to help him buy an anniversary present for his wife and stuff like that, treating me like a kind of niece or something and suddenly I find out he's after my body. Those were his exact words in fact, "I'm after your body," if you can believe anybody would actually say that.

I was stunned for a minute, and then I thought he must be joking, so I just laughed. But then he said, "I've been wanting to throw my arms around you for a long time," and you know for a second I had this picture of a kind of circus act, where I was standing in front of a target, and all these guys would get up on stage, take off their arms and throw them around me, not at me you know? They'd kind of swirl through the air like boomerangs and go in curves right around me.

Anyways, then I said about the fossils and that and got out of the car. Now he hates me too, and not only that I still have to work for him. I mean I was really stupid to say that, I could have trouble with my job. And then to top everything off, the next day this flasher I started telling you about came into the office. I tell you it never rains but it pours.

So anyways, this flasher. He just— Well, I was putting away some files and noticed some guy just standing there trying to catch my eye, and I thought he needed help or something so I just ignored him kind of, you know the way it is when it's busy and you don't want to be bothered. You kind of pretend you don't see them, really. So anyways he stood there for about five minutes before I even noticed! And so finally I looked at him, you know, as if I'd just seen him, and the funny thing was he looked really normal, I mean he didn't look like a perv or anything.

He had kind of short brown hair and was a bit on the skinny side but not short, really. And he wore a nice sports jacket and pants, he wasn't one of those slobs in old jeans or anything and what was the strangest thing—I don't know why I should think this is so weird but I do—he had these stylish glasses on, like the kind Snoopy wears when he's the Red Baron or whatever, only smaller. I really like those glasses. He had a moustache too. And there he was, it was just out, just hanging there like those sausages at Safeway, and this guy had kind of a grin on his face. Jeez I'll never forget it.

I screamed, right? I'd never screamed before in my life, you know. I mean not really, just when I've been at the lake with some guy and he tries to throw me in or stuff like that, just fooling around. Well I really screamed and everybody came hotfooting it to my area and I go something like, I mean I can't remember the exact words, but it was something like, "Call the police this guy's a pervert!"

So that's it. He just stood there in the middle of the room with all these people around, and this big smile on his face, as if he'd won the lottery or something.

Levels of Existence

IN THE SHADE OF THE RESTAURANT'S *CERVEZA* SIGN, ARLENE AND Sheila sipped beer and smoked Fiestas, the second-cheapest Mexican cigarettes. On the other side of the fence, one of the fishermen's wives knelt outside a hut making tortillas on a charcoal-heated griddle. She slapped each tortilla rhythmically from one hand to the other until it was the proper thinness, threw it on the hot griddle for exactly the right amount of time, and piled it on top of the others.

They were sitting so close to her Arlene could see the sweat in the creases of her forehead. She stood up, moved into the light and looked out to sea. The neck and sleeves of her shift were embroidered with flowers which bloomed in almost fluorescent colours. The white cotton of her dress shimmered in the sun and her black, braided hair was the colour of the bluebottle flies buzzing behind the curtains inside the restaurant. A mild breeze from the Caribbean ruffled her dress as she stood outlined against the turquoise sea.

The two young tourists looked at each other. "I wish just once we'd remember to bring the camera," Sheila said.

"Oh, well, we have to get going." Arlene picked up her embroidered denim purse. "It's almost eleven-thirty."

They had walked the mile and a half of beach to the village and missed the supply truck for the second time in a week. They were staying with four other people in a hut down the beach known locally as Chunzibul, which somone had told them means "bark of a tree" in Mayan. Since the truck only came to Playa del Carmen twice a week, Arlene and Sheila knew their friends would not be pleased.

None of them had much money; they all wanted to be able to live on the beach out at Chunzibul for next to nothing. They had met on a second-class bus and heard about the hut from another traveller. The six of them had decided to pool their resources and move in together, if it was still unoccupied.

Arlene and Sheila were glad to be in with a group of other tourists and to be able to stay at a place for free. They were wasting their money by taking buses rather than hitching rides. Hitch-hiking in Mexico had lost its appeal after they'd had to deal with two gropers and a masturbator, all on the same day.

Two fishermen passed the restaurant veranda, leered at them and hissed. Hissing, they had discovered, was the Mexican equivalent of a wolf whistle. "*Mamasita*," the men crooned, puckering their lips in exaggerated Latin kisses, swaggering as if they were enacting a parody.

The village houses were either cement boxes painted in tired pastels or thatched huts with sand floors. There was one hotel, a block of four cement rooms with a restaurant. The rooms were never used except by stranded tourists who missed the ferryboat to the island of Cozumel or Isla Mujeres. Few people stopped at Playa del Carmen by choice, although the beaches were long and white and lined with coconut palms and the Caribbean was as clear and blue here as by the islands. It was, as yet, undiscovered by regular tourists, and the few who had found their way to the beaches down the coast from the village felt like privileged explorers. There was, however, not much to do except lie on the beach, swim, eat and sleep, which had sounded fine to Arlene and Sheila until they tried it for a month.

They lived with two couples, Molly, Ian, Mike and Philippa. Molly and Ian slept in the hut, and the others all slept in a row out on the beach, unless it rained. Each night they watched the stars come out before drifting off to the sound of waves.

Arlene and Sheila became so bored that, for them, Mike had developed the attractiveness of a minor cult figure. Molly and Ian were in love; they were a couple, but Mike and Philippa never slept together, they never made love at all as far as the girls could see. They talked about spirituality. They never wore shoes, they said, even when it was cold; they were teaching their feet to feel. Mike had the aura of mystery, the fascination of an unreachable priest, a celibate mystic. Arlene and Sheila each considered making a play for him, but were hampered by the knowledge that they'd seen better days, as far as being attractive was concerned. A diet of beans, tortillas, buns, fish, coconuts, oatmeal and beer was not conducive to creating svelte bodies, especially since their main passion in the past month, in spite of Mike, was food. One day between the two of them they'd eaten thirty sweet Mexican breadrolls.

They entered the tiny store. "*Buenos días.*"

"*Buenas.*" The storekeeper eyed them balefully. They bought enough supplies to last a couple of days, and counted their change carefully.

By the time they started back, the village was entirely deserted; even the dogs sat in the shade. It was almost high noon. They wrapped scarves on their heads to protect themselves from the sun and began to walk, kicking the fine white-sugar sand that sifted between their toes. They splashed aimlessly in the shallow waves where the sand was hard, the bottoms of their rolled-up jeans becoming soaked. They could see the heat shimmering in waves almost as substantial as the water.

"The guys got to go fishing again didn't they?" Arlene stopped and scraped some beach tar off her feet. "What a piss-off we can't go. At least it would be something to do."

Palm trees lined the white beach, feathery fronds waving in the Caribbean breeze. The water was a vivid turquoise even when the weather was cloudy, and today it sparkled in aquamarine splendour.

"I guess we can always go swimming," Sheila sighed.

♦

Molly and Philippa were sitting under the palm trees beside the hut, reading. Only Mike and Ian were able to go fishing, since it was considered bad luck to allow women on the boats. "And forget not," Philippa quoted as the two shoppers sat beside her, grateful for the shade, "that the earth delights to feel your bare feet/And the winds long to play with your hair."

"Shit is it hot or what," said Arlene.

Sheila gave Arlene a look. She knew she wanted to avoid mentioning the groceries. "We missed the supply truck and had to go to Aguillar's," she said.

"Again?" Molly looked at them with mild disgust. Neither of them had anything at all to do. Nothing at all but to meet the supply truck for groceries. "Oh well," she sighed, "at least Aguillar's has good buns."

"I wish we could find some peanut butter," Arlene said, sifting sand through her fingers.

Ian and Molly were from New York. Molly was thin and dark with long braids. Ian was tall and solid, with a big nose and a crooked smile. They were mature, in their mid-twenties; they'd had real jobs once. Molly told stories about herself and her family. Her father had been a Catholic priest who'd lived five years with her mother before finally giving up the priesthood, becoming a social worker and marrying her. Now Molly's mother wouldn't speak to her because she was living in sin with Ian.

Arlene and Sheila were from Saskatoon, Saskatchewan. They'd been best friends since high school and lived through first-year university together in a basement suite. By the time they finished the fall term of their second year they decided they'd had enough darkness and boredom, took the remainder of their student loan money and went to Mexico for the rest of the winter. Everything had turned out all right so far. Here it was almost the end of April and they still had enough money to get home.

Sheila said this was an adventure that had changed her forever. Arlene was greatly disappointed when she first realized on the beach in Mazatlán she was nobody but herself, nobody but Arlene, with the same old consciousness, viewpoint, everything, walking along the beach eating corn on the cob with hot sauce instead of ploughing through the cold to get to Taverna's for a pizza. She tried to explain this feeling around the fire one evening. She could never understand, she said, why people always talked about finding themselves when she couldn't seem to get rid of herself.

Mike and Philippa had met on the road. Mike was slender and attractive with long red hair that fell in a mass of tangles over his shoulders, and piercing grey-green eyes that changed colour with the sea. He carried nothing with him but a sleeping bag and a toothbrush. He was from Oregon. He had sat down at Philippa's fire one evening when she was camped near the Mayan ruins at Palenque. After drinking a cup of tea, he got up to do his Tai Chi exercises. Philippa watched him perform his slow-motion ballet and decided he could stay with her. She was from Manchester, England, and she knew this was what she'd been looking for in America. It was all right with her if he was seeking purification to prepare himself for a higher existence. She decided that's what she'd been seeking too.

♦

On Friday, Arlene and Sheila finally got to the village in time for the supply truck, although they were among the last to arrive. Women crowded in front of a semitrailer parked in the village square, waiting for their chance to buy fresh produce as well as beans and cornmeal at bargain prices. When they arrived, the girls were greeted with silence. "Heepy *gringa*," was heard in muted tones from various parts of the crowd.

"*Buenos días*," said Arlene pleasantly.

"This happens every time," muttered Sheila. As soon as they started talking, people politely looked away and resumed their own conversations. In front of them stood the woman who lived by the restaurant. She was holding a baby girl who looked at them with huge eyes, trying to decide whether to cry or to smile.

"Look, her ears are pierced!" said Sheila. "Isn't she a little doll." They smiled at the mother. "*Bonita niña*," they said. "What a pretty little girl."

The woman's other children crowded around her, staring at the *gringas*. The baby had decided to smile, and cooed, reaching for Arlene's blonde hair.

"She thinks I'm an angel," Arlene grinned. "Don't you, sweetheart?"

"You belong in a circus," Sheila commented.

The three women came off the truck together, Arlene and Sheila loaded down with fruit and vegetables, jars of jam, sugar, coffee, cookies and canned meat. The Mexican woman had a few packages of beans and cornmeal.

"Shit, how are we going to carry all of this stuff? We should've brought another grocery bag." Arlene was carrying a bunch of bananas in one arm, an open bag of oranges precariously perched on top; on the other arm was a paper bag full of canned goods. Sheila had the hemp grocery bag slung over one shoulder, full of vegetables, more cans, and packages. They realized the woman and her children were following them and laughing. Arlene dropped her load and sank onto the sand. She and Sheila sat, waiting for the family to pass by. Instead of passing, however, they stopped and sat down beside them, the woman speaking earnestly through her smile, giving them unintelligible advice.

"What's she saying? Something about heads," Arlene said, trying to look pleasant.

The woman pointed to Arlene's groceries and dumped the packages out of her own bag. She then rearranged Sheila's, and packed all the groceries into two compact bundles. Demonstrating what she wanted them to do, she took her scarf and wound it into a sausage-thick roll, which she placed on top of her head; on this she put one of the grocery bundles and started to walk with it, gleefully exaggerating the lightness and easiness of this method of transporting goods.

Arlene and Sheila looked at each other, took off their Mexican scarves and tried it. They put the groceries on their heads and practised walking a few yards.

"Hey! This really works. *Muchas gracias*," the girls nodded and smiled broadly. Sheila took a peso out of her purse and pointed from it to the woman's grocery bag.

She shook her head and said, "*Mañana*."

"She means you can bring it back tomorrow."

"No kidding."

They thanked the woman and started off for Chunzibul. It wasn't long, however, before they realized their heads weren't cut out for carrying heavy loads. "Oh well," said Sheila, "at least we have the extra grocery bag."

"God," said Arlene after trudging along in silence, "I was hoping the supply truck would have peanut butter."

♦

That evening the four women sat out on the beach, waiting for Mike and Ian. The sun's last rays caught the ripples on the surface of the water, turning the sea to liquid gold.

"Here come the fishermen," Sheila said. "It looks like the big ones got away." The two guys plodded through the sand, looking sunburned and exhausted.

"How come you're so late?"

"We had to stay out until we caught something, and then there weren't even enough fish to take any home with us." Ian pushed his hair back from his forehead. "They're not going to invite us again I bet. I heard them saying something about us looking like women. Because of our long hair, the Mother Mary thinks there's women on the boat and that's why they aren't catching enough fish."

"That doesn't even make sense." Arlene looked up from sifting sand through her fingers.

"Why not?"

"Well, Jesus had long hair. I mean, Mary sure as hell wouldn't mistake you guys for women when her own kid had long hair. Why don't you mention that?"

"It might be worth a try." He hesitated. "But anyway the real problem is I think a couple of them find us, uh, attractive."

"What?"

"Yeh, especially Mike. Tell them about Manuel," he nudged Mike.

"Aw just forget it," Mike said. "We just won't go fishing any more." He kicked at the sand. "So what's to eat?"

Later, Mike came out to the beach and sat cross-legged in the sand, the setting sun framing him in radiance, his hair forming an aureole around his head as he chanted quietly to himself. Arlene was reminded of the paintings she'd seen in a book called *Old Masters*. "Madonna with Beard," she thought. "What's he saying?" she asked Philippa.

"His mantra."

"I know but what's the word? Om?"

"I have no idea. It's a personal thing." Philippa stepped gracefully through the sand to the cabin. Her hair had turned taffy coloured in the Mexican sun. It was long and thick, and she wore it loose. She was the only one of the four women who couldn't run along the beach comfortably without a bra.

Arlene and Sheila speculated endlessly about the apparent chastity of her relationship with Mike. They hunted for clues to Mike's soul, listening to his opinions about the meaning of life, questioning him about his past and insinuating themselves into his and Philippa's conversations, even though he hadn't done anything unusual or particularly interesting except refrain from having sex. They knew Philippa must just be biding her time.

Arlene sat down on the sand beside Mike, who had ceased chanting and was now staring out to sea. "So how're your feet coming along?" she asked.

The sun had almost set and his eyes were becoming midnight blue. "What?" He looked suspicious.

"Have they learned how to feel yet?"

He smiled, and his face was radiant. "Piss off," he said genially.

They sat watching the waves, Arlene staring off and on at the growing flab bulging over the waist of her jeans and feeling peaceful and slobbish. Maybe she could simply ask him about his relationship with Philippa. She picked at one of her toenails, thinking of ways to introduce the subject, but Mike stood up to do his Tai Chi. Sheila sat down beside her to watch.

When Sheila and Arlene had decided to go to Mexico in January, Arlene's mother made an appointment for her with a psychiatrist and begged her to see him. Instead, they bought student stand-by tickets to San Diego and took off. The only university class Arlene mildly regretted leaving was Philosophy 102. For some reason, she was fascinated by a quote from Heidegger: *The being that exists is man. Man alone exists. Rocks are, but they do not exist. Trees are, but they do not exist. Horses are, but they do not exist. Angels are, but they do not exist. God is, but he does not exist.*

"So in other words," she'd said to Sheila, "consciousness of self is the key to really existing. But then, what's God doing on that list, or angels for that matter? If they existed, wouldn't they be conscious of their own existence? Maybe I don't understand what Heidegger meant at all."

"Maybe," Sheila had said, "you should have read the whole essay."

Mike was performing his Tai Chi with grace and precision, his slim dancer's body outlined against the fading light. Arlene smelled something that reminded her of high school gym class, then realized it was herself. "I stink therefore I am," she said to Sheila. They sat in silence for awhile, still watching Mike. "Maybe we should go home. We can't live here forever, we'll be total vegetables in another week."

"Who said *I think therefore I am* anyway? That guy whose quote you're always going on about?"

"No, it was some French guy; I forget his name." Arlene frowned. "What do you mean 'always going on about'? I've only mentioned it once or twice since we've been here."

"Speaking of the quote," Sheila said, "I'd like to know what's with all this *man* business?"

"What do you mean *man* business?"

"I mean, 'The being that exists is man. Man alone exists.' What kind of shit is that? What about woman? Women are, but they don't exist, right?"

"Jesus, Sheila, you know he means man in the sense of human beings or people."

"Hah. None of those old farts thought of women as people."

"That's not the point. What you do with these guys is take all their ideas and apply them to women, just the same as you do men. Even if they were sexist pigs that doesn't mean everything they ever thought was totally wrong."

"Yes it does."

"You know sometimes you're such a pain I can't believe it." Arlene was so irritated she could feel it in the pit of her stomach.

"Hah. Ad hominem." Sheila had taken Logic 100.

Mike had been holding a position on one foot for five minutes, with Sheila staring at him the whole time. Now she stood up and walked to the water's edge, but instead of wading in, went deliberately up to Mike. She took his face in her hands, putting him off balance, and gave him a long kiss. She led him toward the jungle growth that lurked behind the palm trees, and he went along with her as if he were a small boy being led into an ice cream parlour, his eyes dark and expectant.

Arlene had the presence of mind to pretend nothing unusual was happening when Philippa came out of the hut to join them. "Sheila and Mike went for a walk," she said. She cursed Sheila silently and hoped a snake would get them. It was really time to leave.

The next morning nothing at all seemed to have happened. Ian, who was always the first one up, was cooking porridge and coffee on the old barrel under the thatched lean-to they called the veranda. The iguanas who lived on the roof of the hut scuttled over the corrugated tin. "The patter of little feet," he said as usual, when everyone walked in.

After they'd eaten, they all lounged around the hut for awhile drinking coffee, reading parts of *In Watermelon Sugar* aloud, fantasizing about American food. Mike sat cross-legged in the middle of the room, playing his concave stomach like a pair of bongo drums. Ian belched and stacked the dishes. Molly told a story about how she used to shave her legs, Philippa sat placidly staring off into space, and Sheila and Arlene quietly stuffed themselves with the last of Aguillar's sweet pastry. Licking her fingers, Sheila announced they were going to pack up and take the evening bus from the village as far as Chichén-Itzá, and then see if they could get a ride with some tourists into Mérida. They were ready, she said, to start the journey home.

Mike stopped his bongo drumming and smiled at both of them. "We'll miss you," he said.

♦

Their backpacks felt heavy that evening on the walk to the village. They were almost there before Arlene asked about Mike.

"Well?" she asked.

"Well what?" Sheila grinned.

"Oh come off it. How was it with Mike?"

"Far out."

"What do you mean 'far out'?"

"He's a really cool guy, he makes love just like you'd expect. I mean I didn't reach Nirvana or anything, but."

"Did you ask about him and Philippa?"

"Yes. You know what he said? He said she was such a spiritual person he didn't know how to approach her. He thinks she's so far above the physical that she's a kind of Zen angel. I guess they sort of got started on the wrong foot."

Arlene hesitated. "I guess we don't really have to leave yet if you don't want. Or maybe you wanted to invite him along?" She felt she had to at least say the words, even if she didn't mean them and Sheila knew it.

"God no," Sheila said. "He's in love with Philippa."

The sunset was colouring their faces and hair a vivid shade of rose. "Hey look at us," said Arlene.

"I'm pink therefore I am," said Sheila.

They began to giggle with a kind of helpless inanity. The village was only a few yards past the next palm tree. "Let's stop at the hotel for a beer." Arlene was trying not to dissolve into absolute idiocy.

"I drink therefore I am," Sheila snorted. Their laughter came in short gasps. The hotel owner, prosperous in patent leather and white polyester, walked past them and hissed.

Arlene shouted after him, "You're a dink therefore you are." This struck them as the ultimate in wit, and they almost collapsed on the beach. They staggered into the village, wiping their eyes and gasping. They walked for the last time down the sand road leading to the restaurant, stepped up onto the patio, put their backpacks beside some chairs and tried to recover themselves. The place was empty except for a wizened man in a straw hat who didn't bother to look up from his beans and eggs. A young man in a yellow T-shirt sauntered in for a pack of Fiestas, eyeing the tourists as if they were on sale in a shop window. He put the pack of cigarettes in his right sleeve.

Arlene wiped tears from her eyes. "Why do Mexican men wear pointed shoes?" she asked. Until now, she'd refused to let herself tell this joke. She'd heard it on a bus in San Diego, and knew racism when she saw it.

"I don't know. *Why* do Mexicans wear pointed shoes?" Sheila asked, glancing at the young man with the Fiestas.

"So they can step on cockroaches in corners." This set them off again, snorting and holding their sides. Nobody came to wait on them.

The woman next door came out of her hut to take some clothes off the line. Arlene took the hemp shopping bag out of her backpack and handed it across the fence, trying to control her laughter. "*Muchas gracias,*" she said.

"*Denada,*" the woman smiled. She hung the shopping bag in her doorway and reached up to gather a load of white cotton clothing. She nodded toward the backpacks. "Go home?" she asked.

"*Sí,*" the girls nodded. They finally caught the eye of the waiter, who came slowly onto the patio to take their orders.

"*Vaya con Dios,*" the woman said. The sun had almost disappeared, but was still bright enough to cast a glow on the clean laundry held in her arms.

Putting Things Away

BETH SAT ON THE COUCH, RESTING. HER HOUSE SEEMED PART cocoon, part aquarium. Sounds from the street were muffled, watery light was filtered through two porches and through small piano windows close to neighbouring houses. The house was very old, and the foundation wasn't good. It slanted toward the street so that when her grandchildren came to visit, their toy trucks and cars rolled to the front door as if remote-controlled.

After Franklin had died, she intended to move into a senior citizens' apartment block. She almost put the house up for sale while she was waiting for a suite to come open, but decided she would hold onto it just in case. When her name finally came up on the waiting list, she went down with the agent to look at the one-bedroom suite. It was so small, there was virtually no storage space; the storeroom was big enough to hold an ironing board and a vacuum cleaner; the kitchen was almost non-existent, with a tiny fridge and microwave and no cupboards at all. The bedroom closet was ridiculous: she would have to keep her dresses in plastic dry cleaning bags under her bed. "They must think anyone over sixty-five turns into a midget with no possessions and no appetite," she said to the agent.

"Most of the people here eat out a lot," he said. "There's lots of good, quite inexpensive restaurants in this area. Or you can heat stuff up in the microwave."

"What about all my clothes and dishes? Not to mention my furniture? What if I'd rather cook for myself?"

The agent shrugged, and Beth said, "Cancel it," and walked out.

As she said to her friend Marge, "I'm not going to let them put me in a coffin before I'm even dead."

Instead, she redecorated her house, bought a new couch and carpets, had new treads put on the stairs and new plumbing fixtures installed in the bathroom. Sometimes she spent whole days at a time walking through the house, cleaning floors and furniture that were already spotless. She dusted her few ornaments and china pieces almost every day, and washed them once a week, just for the pleasure of handling them and keeping them at their best. Her favourite was a Dresden piece her mother had managed to salvage from the old country. It was a little shepherdess in a mauve dress, as dainty and exquisite as a violet.

Just now she was having tea and relaxing after vacuuming the carpet. Beiges and creams and greens, those were the colours on sale at the time she was redecorating. And it looked good too, she thought. Cozy and charming, going well with her old dining room set.

Sometimes when she felt tired she thought of death. She had gone through a terrible time at the death of her husband but underneath the sorrow had been a secret relief: she was glad it wasn't her. There was no question of her rather dying than facing life alone. She remembered studying a Greek story in her school days about someone who had been given eternal life but not eternal youth, and he prayed to have his spirit released from his decrepit body, he prayed for death. If she were him, she'd have chosen life, no matter what, unless she were in too much pain.

Lately she'd been having dreams about being sentenced to death, nightmares in which she resigned herself to being hanged or put in the electric chair, but when nothing happened, when the hangman (or woman as was often the case) only hovered around without actually calling her, she had time to think, time to be overcome with despair and terror. It was always so great a relief to wake up after one of these dreams that it would colour her entire day, clarifying the atmosphere, forcing her to see things in sharp outline and perceive details she wouldn't normally notice.

But she began to be afraid of going to sleep, and sometimes would lie for half the night thinking, remembering all the dead and their deaths: her parents, her husband, her last child, who everyone had said was better off; her friends, more of whom seemed to be dropping off like caricatures of old people in rocking chairs, their heads bowed, chins almost touching their breastbones.

She remembered her mother's death as being a revelation to her. Before then, she hadn't realized anyone really close to her could die. She had felt she and the people in her world were indestructible. During the months when she nursed her mother, her family listened for death as if it were an entity they'd be able to hear stumbling through the doorway. She remembered that time as being weighted with a chain, a necklace of sorrow strung with odd moments of bitterness, love, anger, even funny incidents during which they'd all laughed with a hilarity she'd rarely experienced since. Although her mother's dying came as a relief, it left Beth with a feeling she was afraid, for awhile, would be permanent. She would be walking down the street or going into the kitchen thinking of ordinary things, when the remembrance of her mother's non-existence would cause the street or floor under her to gape open like a fresh wound and she would start falling. It always lasted only a split second and she always dealt with it immediately. Eventually it almost disappeared.

Her husband and her father had both died suddenly and she'd had no nursing to do, no sitting at bedsides holding hands, no waiting. In a way, though, their deaths had been harder on her; they were more of a shock. She'd had no time to let them know anything, no time to prepare.

The periods of grief immediately after any of the deaths had given her a new understanding of religion. She didn't believe in God or in any afterlife, but she realized how easy it would be, how comforting to think that all the dead would be in some down-filled heaven or floating around in space, looking in on her every once in awhile. She discovered, too, why kneeling is a standard religious practice. When waves of intense grief came over her, she always wanted to fall to her knees. From such a position it seemed only natural, she thought, to invent some deity or another to be subordinate to.

She knew, however, even during the worst times, that she had too much common sense to be truly religious, and if she ever weakened and prayed, she would be ashamed of herself after. She knew she was capable of developing her own self-protection; she didn't need the church. She was able to put things away.

She still, for example, never thought of the child. She had the pain of his death wrapped, somewhere inside herself, in layers of gauze she would never unravel. Sometimes he would come to her in dreams, smiling, his slanted eyes glowing in his freckled face. But even after so long a time she knew better than to think about his death. She knew she'd never have the strength to pull herself out if once she allowed herself to fall into that chasm. She did sometimes dwell on the grieving period after, the well-meaning cruelty of those who said it might have been a blessing in disguise.

Others found the thought of the loss of a child, retarded or not, so horrible they avoided her as if she were cursed; they had no idea what to say to her. She had seen her friend Nancy the day after his death, and Nancy had stopped short, turned around and ran, not even attempting a pretence of not noticing her. Nancy never forgave herself, and so of course couldn't forgive Beth; otherwise they might still see each other off and on, since they lived in the same city all these years.

Beth sighed; thirty years. Of course it wasn't only Nancy's fault that they'd lost contact. Beth had resented even the friends who gave her comfort. She hated them all for a time because of their calm lives and healthy children, but she knew enough to deal with those feelings by herself. She pretended, whenever she saw her friends, that her life was going along much like theirs, which in fact, she realized now, was true.

Eventually the bitterness disappeared; only the pain remained and that had to be put away, or it would have taken over her life. The fact that she had other children was, as everyone said, a blessing, partly because they kept her so busy she didn't have time to break down. Franklin was working for the city then in Wascana Park, and seemed to have succeeded in diminishing his sorrow in a short time: clipping it with the grass, trimming it down to size along with the trees. One day he said, "Maybe it was for the best. How would we have handled him if he'd grown up?" She never really forgave him for saying that, but had put it away too, somewhere along with the other unforgivables.

That's what you do in a marriage, she thought, put all the unpardonable words and acts away and go on as if they weren't there. That's the problem with young people, they don't know how to put things away; they keep handling them, turning them over, bringing them out to be aired and rejuvenated. Before they know it they've psychoanalyzed and therapized themselves out of their marriage. She was thinking of her daughter, Louise.

Beth had liked Louise's first husband, but this new one, Charles, was different. She rarely visited them now; Charles obviously found her irritating and tiresome, and she had been hurt, not only by his sarcasms, but by the fact that he thought she didn't get any of them.

Soon after Charles and Louise were married, she'd had them over for supper. Charles sat at the head of the table, a small man who in a few years would become pudgy. Not fat; he didn't, she thought, have the generosity of physique or personality for that. He would merely be pudgy. He prided himself on being witty, and when Beth was too nervously preoccupied with cooking and serving the meal to react with more than surprised awkwardness to his remarks, he became overbearing and caustic. This caused her to become more acutely uncomfortable and the evening had been a disaster. Their relationship had not improved with time.

Now Louise usually came to visit by herself or with the children, and Beth avoided Charles at any family gatherings, except for a few polite exchanges. She had never, of course, said anything about Charles to Louise. Again, she had covered her dislike, put it out of the light before it grew too big to handle.

She rose from the couch and put the vacuum cleaner in the closet, feeling tired, wondering what she'd do if it ever came to the point where she couldn't look after the house. Cross that bridge when she came to it, she guessed.

She wished Franklin were alive. She wanted to touch someone so bad at times that she was afraid. It wasn't sex, although she supposed that was part of it. She needed, simply, to hold and touch and kiss and be kissed. That was all over, except for the hugs and pecks on the cheek she received from her children and grandchildren. Maybe she should get a cat. She'd heard that senior citizens who owned pets had healthier mental outlooks and perhaps even lived longer than those without them. She sat down and wondered if a cat purring on her lap would make much of a difference. She smiled to herself, remembering a kitten she'd received for her seventh birthday, and fell asleep on the couch.

She knew it was mid-afternoon when she woke up because that was the only time the sun's rays could shine through the side window onto her snake plant. She still felt drowsy but forced herself up; she didn't want to let herself get lazy. She sat for a few seconds feeling something was strange but couldn't focus on what it could be. When she tried to stand, she collapsed onto the carpet. What on earth, she thought. She was more confused than frightened and couldn't understand what was happening. She forced herself to concentrate and realized she had no feeling on her left side, including the side of her face. She knew what to do, she just couldn't let herself panic. She had to get to the phone and dial. Was it 199 or 911? She remembered a man in a TV movie yelling, "Dial 911! Dial 911!" because someone was drowning in his swimming pool. That was all she let herself think, 911, 911. Moving each inch exhausted her, and it seemed to take a lifetime, but she was finally able to pull the telephone off the table and dial. She was not able to say, "Ambulance." She was not able to say anything.

She was conscious when the police and ambulance people found her, and remained so throughout the trip to the hospital. She must now be someone else, she felt, someone for whom sirens wail. She couldn't be Beth anymore. Beth was somewhere else, watching. Ask not for whom the sirens wail, they wail for thee. Was that witty, she wondered. Would Charles appreciate that one? She felt herself blacking out as they were wheeling her into Emergency.

She woke up in a narrow bed, swathed in white and hospital green. She still felt as if she were someone else and kept wondering when this woman's body would begin to function properly again. She didn't want herself to be in other people's hands. Where am I? she wondered, and now she understood why it was such a cliché, why it was common for people to ask that question on regaining consciousness in a hospital bed. She meant: Where is Beth? Where am I?

Maybe she was dying; she felt a moment of terror. I've got to get hold of myself, she thought. And again she realized the double meaning: she was not here, she had to get hold of herself. Ha, to find herself, like the hippies in the sixties. Oh God.

Louise was by the bed, looking haggard and worried and ready to cry. When she saw Beth was awake she leaned across the bed and kissed her. "Jerry and Lorene are on their way," she said. "They should be here this morning."

Is there going to be a scene, Beth wondered. A death scene, with her children gathered by her bedside? Charles came in, looking, she thought, appropriately serious, holding a bouquet of flowers.

She struggled to speak, but all she could produce was a strangled garble. This woman can't even talk, she thought.

Charles and Louise looked at each other. Beth could see they knew something they weren't saying aloud. "She can't talk at all," Louise said.

"She'll be better in awhile," he said, touching Louise's arm. "Maybe she's just exhausted." He turned to Beth. "You'll be okay once you've had some more rest, eh Beth?" He spoke loudly, enunciating each syllable. He turned gently to Louise, not waiting for an answer. "She should go back to sleep," he said.

At least, Beth thought, he's concerned about Louise. He's never had anything to do with death, she realized. He's unsure of the way to be, has no idea of the emotional protocol.

She looked around the room. Everything, the loose thread hanging from her blanket, the highly polished tiles out in the hallway, the little holes in the white ceiling, had become finely delineated like the subjects in the realistic art her son had taken her to see last time he'd been in town. She felt she could lie there forever and not be bored; she found everything fascinating. She stared at the bouquet of carnations and daisies Charles was still holding awkwardly, and noticed each pollen-covered stamen and pistil, the design on every petal.

She was relieved that she didn't feel afraid any more. She looked at Charles and didn't dislike him at all. He was nothing but another person who meant well, a man going through life being good enough. This was going to be hard on Louise, she thought, but didn't feel any more for the woman sitting next to the bed than for the flowers they were finally putting in a hospital vase. Isn't that strange, she thought. That woman with lines around her eyes is my daughter. She had the same feeling now that she had whenever she finished house cleaning. Everything was clean, dusted and polished, and she could rest.

But then she felt different again; she felt herself coming back, that it was really her, Beth, who was now in this bed, in this hospital. So this is me, dying, she said to herself, and was engulfed in an unexpected rush of misery, an overpowering sense of loss. She would lose everybody. She'd never see her grandchildren grow up; her friends and children would go on living, without her. Her house would be sold. For her, she realized, everything was dying. Sadness became an almost physical pain. "I can't bear it," she tried to say aloud, forgetting she couldn't make herself understood.

Louise smoothed her forehead, "It's okay, Mom," she said. "I'm still here."

Beth longed for the apathy she'd felt moments before, but knew the sorrow would be there from now on, standing solidly by her bed like one of the Wild Things she used to read about to her grandchildren when they were small, only whispering to her, grey and monumental. She would barter her soul to believe in an afterlife, she thought, and grimaced, almost producing a smile.

After all, she thought, she'd been compromising all her life, why couldn't she just let go about this one thing, convince herself that maybe there was the possibility. But no. She'd been able to fool herself about all kinds of things, but not this. She just knew better, and that was it.

She wanted to weep, to wail and cry herself to death, but she'd always avoided making scenes and didn't have the strength to begin now. She lay still, gazing out the window feeling as fragile as her Dresden china piece. She closed her eyes and thought if only someone would shut the curtains, maybe she could go back to sleep. Maybe she could just put everything away.

"Here's that minister again," Charles said, in the same tone the kids used to say, "That salesman is here again," or, "It's those Jehovah Witnesses at the door, Mom." The minister poked his head in the room and introduced himself. He was in his forties, with a longish fringe of hair, a checked shirt under a sober sports jacket, and round cheeks beaming with social enthusiasm. Beth could picture exactly what he'd looked like when he was seven. He reminded her somehow of her little boy, before he'd become ill.

"May I be of any help?" he asked. There was a short silence before he said, "Perhaps she'd like me simply to read from the Bible, and you two could go for a coffee break if you wished, or . . . ?" His voice faded away, as Charles and Louise shook their heads. Beth struggled to say something, and managed a slight nod. They looked at each other in surprise, and eventually went out, saying they'd be back in a few minutes.

The minister sat down and read through a list of psalm and prayer titles until Beth nodded again.

"The Lord is my shepherd; I shall not want," he began, but before he reached the part about the valley of the shadow of death, his words ceased to penetrate Beth's consciousness. All she could hear was sorrow whispering, and then a sudden sharp memory of Franklin reading to Louise's oldest boy when he was three or four: " . . . and he sailed off through night and day and in and out of weeks and almost over a year to where the wild things are."

♦

Life Skills

♦

I DON'T LIKE NIGHT DRIVING. THE ONCOMING LIGHTS DON'T IMPAIR my vision, exactly, but they impair my ability to judge. I can't tell, for example, if a light is a few metres or a few hundred metres away, and I'm never altogether sure on which side of the highway headlights are travelling or even whether they're moving at all. Besides this, I have a horror of smashing into the rear end of a stalled car in the dark, so every time I see two red dots on the highway in front of me, I slow down.

I'm driving home now, Saturday night, because my husband, Carter, wants me to come to his class party tomorrow evening. Otherwise I would have stayed at the farm with my dad for the weekend, since the relatives who came to the family reunion will be dropping in all day tomorrow to take a look at the old homestead, and he'd have appreciated some help. Then again, my help wouldn't be much more than moral support, since I never bake goodies and Dad can make coffee as well as anybody. Anyway, Carter is still in Regina finishing his course, and our daughter, Lynne, is staying for a few days with some cousins we met at the reunion.

I was disappointed that Carter couldn't come with me. He's popular with most of my relatives, especially the older aunts. He has a courtly, charming manner with old ladies that he never bothers to bring out for anyone else. When I said he could at least make an effort to get the weekend off, he became immediately defensive. "I told you," he said, "this isn't an ordinary weekend. We're doing evaluations."

"But Aunt Signe will be really disappointed not to see you; she thinks you're God's gift to women. Of course, compared to either of her husbands you probably are."

"You're the one who's always saying you have nothing in common with most of your relatives. You don't want to go to the reunion either, you just want me to come along and suffer too."

"Speaking of suffering, what about the time I put up with your Aunt Jennifer and Uncle Farley staying with us for two weeks. I mean how does that compare with one lousy afternoon with my relatives?"

He looked disgusted. "You tell me, Elaine. How does it compare? Not to mention the fact that Jen and Farley stayed with us four years ago."

"You could at least take one day off," I said. "I mean how can you evaluate life skills anyway?"

"I told you, we're learning how to *teach* people life skills. God you're thick sometimes."

"Ha. What happened to those techniques you're learning? Is 'God you're thick' one of the terms of—"

"Ah for Christ's sake leave it alone," he interrupted.

Well. So I left it alone. I'm surprised that he wanted me to come to the party, since we weren't on actual speaking terms until just before he went back to Regina last Sunday. I certainly don't feel like going, but I think for some reason it's important I be there. In fact, I felt the same way about the family reunion, and I'm glad I went to that, so there you go. You just never know.

♦

The Sigurdson family reunion was almost entirely organized by Ripplings, a family one of my more prolific aunts married into. The Ripplings practically outnumber the combined forces of the Sigurdsons and that, along with the fact that most of our family are notoriously unenthusiastic about attending social occasions, made me expect a poor turnout. I was surprised, then, when my father and Lynne and I got to the Crystal Creek Legion Hall and there was a big crowd. Aunt Signe made a beeline for me the minute she noticed we were there.

"It's a real shame your brother and his family couldn't make it. Doreen and I were just saying we can't understand all these young people traipsing all over the world."

"Well," I said, "they're not exactly traipsing, Aunt Signe. Jeff is working on a water development project and Marcy is teaching."

"Yes dear I know, the hippie days are over, touch wood," she said, and tapped her knuckles on her forehead. "Nobody your age is travelling around much any more."

"That's because we're all middle-aged I guess."

Aunt Signe snorted. "You? Middle-aged?" She looked around absent-mindedly. "Now, where's your dad got to?"

"He's over there with Uncle Elwood, showing off all those pictures Jeff sent from Swaziland."

"Swaziland?" She looked vaguely confused. "Oh, that's where he's working? Well I'll certainly have to see those snapshots. It's one of those Arab countries, isn't it?"

"Uh, no, it's in Africa. It's near South Africa, I mean. They're finding it really interesting, and the climate—"

"Elaine," she interrupted. "I thought Carter was with your dad but I don't see him. Is he here?"

"He couldn't make it, he's taking a course and they're doing evaluations this weekend."

"Oh I knew he was taking a course, I just thought he'd get an important weekend like this off. Elwood was saying something about the course; what was it called again?"

"Uh, life skills."

"Oh, yes, that's what Elwood said. He said it doesn't take much skill to live until you reach his age." We both smiled. Something caught her eye across the room, and she said, "Oh, did you know Lorne's here?"

"Lorne?" I said, pleased that there was at least someone here with whom I could have a reasonable conversation. "Well for heaven's sake, where is he? You know, we've been to see him a couple of times when we were down east for holidays."

"Have you? Is he still split up with his wife?"

"Oh, he's been divorced for years now. I never really knew her at all."

"There he is," Signe pointed, "talking to— Who is that? Oh, Alma Ogle. Isn't she living in the States now?"

My cousin Lorne hadn't been home since the death of his brother Dwayne in a car accident ten years ago. I remember relatives furtively talking about alcohol "being involved," as if it had been a lover, an unauthorized person found in the car, like Ted Kennedy's secretary at Chappaquiddick. Anyway, there was Lorne looking dazed and slightly desperate so I manoeuvred my way over to save him from Alma, who my brother once described as suffering from Partzheimer's Disease. "I just can't get over it," she was saying. "There must've been some mistake somewhere, that's for sure."

"Uh, I'm not sure what . . . "

"Oh wait a minute, now I know who you are." I could almost see a light bulb flash above her head. "You're Lorne, not Dwayne."

"Well, yes." Lorne ceased to look perplexed and became merely uncomfortable.

"Well no wonder you're alive then."

"Uh, yes. It was Dwayne who had the accident."

"That was such a shame. I heard about it just after we moved to Philadelphia. Such a shame."

I said my hellos during the awkward pause that followed, and gave Alma a chance to escape. "I really must get busy and help Signe with the coffee," she said, "so I think I'll leave you and Lorne to talk about old times." She wandered off into the crowd, still talking. "My goodness, isn't this a madhouse?"

"What do you think, Elaine," Lorne said, a grin transforming his face, "is there anywhere a person can get a drink here?"

"Are you kidding? You must have been gone even longer than I thought if you think you can get a drink at a Rippling get-together."

"Oh well. Just thought I'd ask. Remember that summer you worked in Saskatoon and borrowed my ID to get into the Ritz?"

"God. I used to say my name was Lorna and they'd made a spelling mistake on my driver's licence, or at least that's what I was going to say if the question came up."

"Jeez, I wonder if they still serve green beer on St. Patrick's Day?"

"I'm afraid the Ritz doesn't even exist any more."

He looked shocked for a moment. "No. Really? Jeez, that's kind of depressing."

We were both quiet for awhile, thinking of Dwayne. He used to go to the Ritz a lot. "How are you anyway, Lorne?" I said. "I mean, are you okay now?" I was thinking of the last time we'd visited him; he'd been hitting the bottle pretty hard.

"Oh sure. Yeh, really, I'm just fine. It's kind of weird coming home again and all that, though. I mean coming back to Crystal Creek after all these years and feeling the same as when I was still in school. Like as if Grant Boychuck was going to yell my nickname at me from across the street."

"I know."

"Or as if all the relatives are still worried I'm going to turn out to be a shiftless hippie even though I've been working steady for eighteen years."

"God. Eighteen years? Now I really feel old."

"But I mean, here we'll be I bet, twenty years from now at the next reunion and we'll feel the same and so on for the rest of our days. Maybe none of us ever really leaves home."

"Huh. I remember sitting in the Ritz thinking well this is it. I've left Crystal Creek for good and now my real life is beginning."

Lorne made a face. "Real life," he said.

"Well, in a way I was right. I mean I would never move back to a small town of any kind, let alone Crystal Creek. God, just the thought gives me a pain."

"Funny, though, in spite of everything I'm glad I made it out here in time for the weekend."

"You know, Lorne, when I first saw you across the hall I thought you looked just like your dad. You were standing just like him."

"Hm." He looked at me and smiled. "You don't look like anybody, as far as I can see."

Lorne and I are members of the introverted side of the family. I figured out by the time I was twelve that there are no in-betweens in my father's relatives: you're either an introvert or an extrovert. Most of the immigrant generation were teetotalling introverts. The ones who married extroverts seem to have had outgoing children who are community minded, and the ones who married other introverts produced shy offspring, most of whom drink.

I also noticed, as a child, that the introverts were mostly on the tall, thin side, and the extroverts short and stocky, and the phenomenon struck me again as I looked across the hall. The extroverts were buzzing around organizing food distribution, introducing people, making announcements (there was to be an amateur hour later in the afternoon). The introverts hung around the sides or in corners like poorly rooted flowers, looking insecure but pleased, waiting for others to come to them, as Lorne and I were doing until he moved off in search of coffee, and my cousin Sheri came over.

Sheri and I have been friends since we were babies. An old photo album at home has a picture of her and me as toddlers in snowsuits. I'm bending so that my hood hides my face, and I'm telling Sheri a secret. Her little face is intent: listening and concerned.

"Uncle Elwood says Carter's taking a course? Something called 'Skills for the Living'?"

"Very funny." I was getting tired of hearing Elwood's comments second-hand. "He's a real card."

"Who," Sheri teased, "Elwood or Carter?"

"Well ha." I said. "Certainly not Carter."

"What do you mean, certainly not Carter? How's the class going, anyway?"

"I don't want to talk about it. He's tuned in and turned on to I'm okay you're okay. His classmates give each other strokes and warm fuzzies."

"Oh Elaine they do not."

"No kidding! You know what they have to do? Take turns telling the group about a traumatic experience. It was Carter's turn this week and he wasn't sure what he was going to talk about. He said all the others cried during their stories."

"It sounds, uh, pretty intensive."

"I asked him whether he'd still get his certificate if he didn't cry. He said maybe he'd talk about the day we got married; that would do the trick."

"Now that's more like Carter."

"Yeh. Except if he did something like that he'd get low marks for poor attitude and then I'd be mad at him for wasting time and money."

Sheri looked thoughtful. "Actually, it sounds a bit like they're using some of the stuff that was in this marriage enrichment course Dan and I took through the church last year. This kind of thing can really help you to become a broader person you know."

I smiled, noticing Sheri hadn't lost any weight since we'd last seen each other.

"And quit grinning like that. I know I'm getting fat."

"Oh you are not, you look just fine. Anyway, you can't compare one weekend of consciousness-raising with your own husband to a six-week exercise in group hugging with a bunch of strangers."

"It can't be that bad."

"No really. I think what's happening is, they're in such an intensive situation that it's like being brainwashed. That pop psychology stuff can be as bad as born-again Christians or the Moonies."

Sheri grinned. "Remember when you got interested in joining that witches' coven from Lumsden? We all thought you'd flipped right out that time."

"Come on, I was nineteen then."

"Jeez, all the stuff we used to get into. If our parents only knew eh?"

"By the way, where are *our* offspring? I haven't been able to keep track of Lynne since we got here."

"Can't you see her, over there by the door? In fact, there's Jason playing with her. Oh, now that I think of it, he and Natalie were wondering if Lynne could come and stay with us for a few days."

I hesitated. She's never been away from home before for longer than overnight. "I guess it's up to her if she wants to. Dan can drive her home when he's in Saskatoon next week, eh?"

"Yes, that's just how we planned it." Sheri's expression changed, almost imperceptibly. "Here's Mom," she said.

Aunt Irene came up to us, almost literally beaming. "I swear, you both look about twelve years old to me and here you are, thirty-five."

Sheri rolled her eyes at me, just as she used to when we were adolescents. "Why don't you broadcast it over the sound system, Mom," she said.

"Tsk. As if everybody here didn't know how old you are. Well of course, maybe twelve is pushing it a little. But really, you actually look better now than when you were both flower children sitting around listening to that *music*, and quoting from that book. Oh what was it— You know that hippie poetry book with all the quotes?"

"Rod McKuen?" Sheri ventured.

I was horrified. "No. I've never read Rod McKuen."

"You did. Don't you remember when you had that crush on Jerry Doherty?"

"Oh God."

"Oh I know, Mom's talking about *The Prophet*. Remember? 'Give your hearts, but not into each other's keeping.'"

"'For only the hand of Life can contain your hearts.'" I made a face. "Can you believe it?"

Irene looked a bit impatient with our trip down memory lane. "Anyway Elaine," she said, "where's your husband?"

"He's in Regina taking this course in life skills for his adult education classes. They're doing evaluations this weekend."

"Life skills?" She looked as if I'd said Carter was taking embroidery.

"Really, it's not very interesting."

Sheri cut in. "You know, Mom. It's to do with Carter's work: psychology stuff to help people find jobs and that."

"Well Carter doesn't need a job again does he?"

"No, no," I said, "he's supposed to *teach* this stuff in the fall. His college made the course a requirement. Actually, I don't even know what it is. All I know is I'll be glad when it's over."

"Oh well." Irene patted my arm. "A few weeks living apart is nothing. Just imagine what truck drivers' wives have to put up with."

It's not Carter's absence that's driving me crazy, however, but his enthusiasm. I expected him to come home on weekends making fun of it all, and instead he's been trying out new techniques for handling marital confrontations. Last Saturday, for example, we had one of our usual exchanges about him not finding his wallet. Sometimes we have the exact same conversation, only reversed, when I lose my purse.

"Elaine. Where's my wallet? I can never find anything in this house, it drives me crazy. Elaine! Where's my wallet!"

"How the hell should I know? What are you, in kindergarten, you can't even look after your own stuff?"

Instead of continuing his search and finding his wallet in his jacket pocket as usual, he came into the room looking sanctimonious. "Please," he said, his hand pushing down the air in front of him, "*may* we talk about this."

I couldn't believe it. "Talk about what?" I asked. "Losing your *wallet?* The only life skill you're learning is how to be a pompous ass."

♦

I don't think anything Carter has ever done before has upset me as much as him taking this course so seriously, and really, I can't understand why. God knows his various obnoxious moods and habits have made me miserable enough at times, but there's always been his sense of humour and the fact that I can be just as awful in my own way, which maintains a kind of balance. But when he wants to sort out our relationship to suit a formula, when he's actually in earnest about some kind of drivel encouraging people to "get in touch with themselves," I feel betrayed, as if he's become someone I wouldn't have considered marrying. It must be like this for someone whose spouse suddenly sees the light and gets religion.

I sat through most of the amateur hour at the family reunion thinking about it. The Ripplings are a religious family, and a large percentage of the entertainment was made up of hymns sung in three-part harmony.

Right at the beginning when the M.C., one of my Rippling cousins, took the stage, I knew what we'd be in for. "The first act of our show today," he said after testing the microphone, "will be Jane, Miriam and Garnet Rippling singing, uh what are you singing, kids? Three hymns? Oh. Okay. Here they are folks, give them a big welcome."

"*Jesus bids us shine with a pure clear light,/ Like a little candle burning in the night./ In this world of darkness, so let us shine,/ You in your small corner and I in mine.*"

I was still sitting between Sheri and Lorne an hour and a half later, twiddling my thumbs and wishing I were outside playing with the kids, when the M.C. introduced my daughter and Sheri's two children as part of the entertainment. They sang "God Sees the Little Sparrow Fall" without a trace of shyness, grinning at our surprise, and when they were finished, bowing like little vaudeville troupers. They sounded really quite awful, I suppose, and I have no idea where Lynne learned the words to that hymn. Still, I was transported with pride; Sheri and I nudged each other and got all teary-eyed. Lorne thought they were hilarious and we were mad at him.

I truly wished Carter was there, and I was glad I was going to the life skills party, so I could see him right away to tell him about it.

I think now that one of the reasons I feel I should go to the party is the same as why I went to the reunion: because I am a member of a family. The fact that someone other than myself encouraged my child to perform in the family entertainment has left me feeling not only guilty, but bereft, somehow. I think all of us Sigurdsons, the introverts, that is, have the feeling that we should be excused; that we're special people who should be allowed to hang around the sidelines and observe. We feel entitled to the privilege of being self-absorbed. I realize the older I get, the more like that I'm becoming.

Everyone agreed that the reunion was a resounding success. Afterward, I left my father and my daughter sitting around the kitchen table at the farm with Sheri's and Elwood's families. Dad and Elwood sat, quiet as usual but looking pleased with their world, just as they had looked years ago when my mother was still living and I had just come back from a trip to Europe. The kitchen is now painted a cream colour, but back then it was shiny white, with red chairs around a grey arborite table, and the Middle East was on the news from the radio on top of the fridge. My mother was shelling peas by the counter, and I sat with Dad and Elwood at the table drinking coffee. "Huh," my dad said, "with all the trouble down in those countries, gas is going to go up again."

"You know," I said, "I was only in Israel for a month, but I really got the impression the only thing holding the country together is the fact that the Arabs give the people a common enemy."

"Could you pass the cream, Elaine?"

Elwood took another sugar lump. "The price of pigs's gone down," he said. "We should've sold last week."

"Well," my dad shook his head. "You just never know."

"*Well.*" Uncle Elwood stirred his coffee. "That's a deep hole in the ground."

And then they both looked absent-mindedly in my direction and smiled, on me, I realized, not at me. They had no idea they were being rude, or even that I expected a response. It was enough for them that I was healthy and that I was home.

I have my own view of my world, too, and I'm not tolerant of having it changed. I know Carter's course isn't entirely ridiculous. It teaches people to help others cope with practical real-life skills too, such as how to fill out forms, open accounts, deal with officials, manage money, find jobs.

Actually, I have problems with most of the above, and could use some instruction in life skills myself. For that matter, Carter and I could use some sure-fire techniques for dealing with marital confrontation, and I realize he probably just thought what the heck, it can't hurt to try just about anything.

I, however, seem to have lost the desire to try anything. Since I lost interest in the occult and no longer quote Kahlil Gibran, I've become increasingly satisfied with what goes on in my own self: I'm satisfied I have more common sense than most people I know, in spite of my lack of life skills. In fact, I realize, I've become smug, just like my dad and uncle, and likely just as hard to live with. But so what? Carter isn't exactly perfect himself.

♦

Even though I've become more or less resigned to it, I'm not looking forward to the life skills party. I've met the instructor. He radiates good fellowship and looks you straight in the eye. His handshake is very firm and lasts just a shade longer than expected. Many of the students are women who, as Carter says, are either pre- or post-divorsal. I can picture them hovering like vulture hens, ready to comfort the more attractive men after their descriptions of traumatic experiences.

Carter is quite capable of deciding to hell with it at the last minute and actually describing our wedding day. He kept my family entertained for an entire Christmas dinner once, going into details of how his knees had knocked together, how chills had gone up and down his spine. He described particular events from his life as they'd passed before his eyes during the ceremony. My dad laughed so hard he choked on a piece of turkey and had to have his back pounded.

I suppose I should be thankful Carter wants me to attend the party at all. "So," he said, as he was looking for clean socks to take with him to Regina, "are you coming to the life skills party next weekend or what?" This was the day after the incident with the wallet.

I stared off into space and considered the tone of the question.

"Elaine, do you ever listen to one single thing I say?"

"I heard you already. I was just considering whether I should go or not. It seems pretty strange to me that none of the other spouses are going."

"Well as you know, this type of thing can put a strain on relationships." He smiled; he had decided to relax and was being only mildly sarcastic. "Not everybody's as open-minded as you."

"Ah, what the heck," I answered in the same tone, "why not? Maybe I'll take one small step towards getting in touch with myself. Maybe I'll find out, I mean who knows; maybe I'll find out that I'm okay!"

"I wouldn't count on it if I were you," he said.

♦

So I'm on my way home, and tomorrow I'll go on to Regina to the party. At least I'll be able to drive in the daylight. As I said before, I'm not used to night driving and it makes me nervous. The dark highway seems to be travelling with me, catching up and passing at intervals, the same white lines shining again and again in my headlights. Once or twice already I've forgotten to dim my lights, and the oncoming vehicles have flashed their brights in my eyes, as a reminder.

Marlis Wesseler

Marlis Wesseler has published and broadcast a number of her short fiction and dramatic pieces. A monologue, "Exposing," which was later retitled "Indecent Exposure," won Twenty-Fifth Street Theatre's Annual Short Play Writing Contest in 1988. Wesseler has also been commissioned to write a series of children's plays and a radio drama by CBC Radio.

Wesseler was born, raised, and educated in Saskatchewan. She has an honours degree in English from the University of Regina and also holds her professional teaching certificate. She lives in Regina with her husband Lutz and son Evan.

Michael Gilbert

Michael Gilbert is an award-winning professional photographer whose work has appeared in many countries. While his home base is currently in Hawaii, he maintains a studio in Toronto.

New Fiction from Coteau Books

Other titles in the McCourt Fiction Series are listed below. You may purchase or order any of these titles from your favorite bookstore. For a complete catalogue of publications—fiction, poetry, drama, criticism, non-fiction, and children's literature—please write to Coteau Books at 401-2206 Dewdney Avenue, Regina, Saskatchewan S4R 1H3.

The McCourt Fiction Series

Sun Angel by Chris Fisher. McCourt Fiction Series 8. Compassionate and sometimes humorous stories of small town life.
$12.95(pbk) ISBN 1-55050-039-2

Life Skills by Marlis Wesseler. McCourt Fiction Series 7. A richly textured story collection of women's voices with international settings.
$12.95(pbk) ISBN 1-55050-040-6

The Bonus Deal by Archie Crail. McCourt Fiction Series 6. Stories rooted in South Africa's heritage of apartheid.
$12.95(pbk) ISBN 1-55050-031-7; $24.95(hc) ISBN 1-55050-032-5

Women of Influence by Bonnie Burnard. McCourt Fiction Series 5. Named Best First Book in the Commonwealth Writers Prize, 1989. In its third printing.
$10.95(pbk) ISBN 0-919926-82-7

The Wednesday Flower Man by Dianne Warren. McCourt Fiction Series 4. Witty and whimsical fiction.
$10.95(pbk) ISBN 0-919926-68-1

Night Games by Robert Currie. McCourt Fiction Series 1. Poignant stories about adolescence in the fifties.
$7.00(pbk) ISBN 0-919926-19-3